Dougal Daley

I'm Phenomenal

More books by
Jackie Marchant

Dougal Daley – It's not My Fault!

Dougal Daley – Where's My Tarantula?

Dougal Daley

I'm Phenomenal

WACKY BEE

This edition published in 2018 by Wacky Bee Books
Shakespeare House, 168 Lavender Hill, London SW11 5TG
www.wackybeebooks.com

ISBN 978-0-9956972-6-3

British Library Cataloguing in Publication Data
A CIP catalogue record for this book is available
from the British Library

Internals designed by Ali Ardington

Printed and bound in the UK by Clays Ltd, Elcograf S.p.A.

For Rosie – JM

For Daniel and Sophie – LS

To Mr Truss – it wasn't my fault! – DD

Note from the author – no
Horned Lizards were harmed in
the making of this book!

CONTENTS

GROUNDED

I, Dougal Daley, star goalkeeper for Fairford United and local hero, have been most unfairly grounded — again. It's my teacher's fault, for writing a letter to my parents. Here it is:

OCKLESFORD JUNIOR SCHOOL

Duty Road, Ocklesford, Middx

Dear Mr and Mrs Daley,

I am very sorry to be writing to you again, but I have sent several letters to you on this matter and have not had a reply. I have tried contacting you by phone and text, but the school office appears to have the wrong contact details for you. One number went through to a Chinese takeaway and the other to a competition which cost me 50p a second and I didn't win. I have tried emailing you at <u>LuckyParentsofDougalDaley@hotmail.com</u>, but I received an error message in return. It appears such an email does not exist.

This is a FINAL REMINDER that your son, DOUGAL DALEY, should have completed his ICT project two weeks ago. When I asked him why he hadn't finished it, he said the dog ate it. This project was completed at school during ICT sessions and, unless your dog has been eating our computers, I cannot accept this as an excuse.

Please ensure that Dougal completes his ICT project at home over the weekend and brings it to school on a USB stick on Monday. I trust the dog will not swallow the USB stick. Might I suggest you watch Dougal to make sure he doesn't feed it to the dog like his homework?

Yours sincerely,

Mr E Truss

PS – please could you also ask Dougal to complete his maths homework?

PPS – please could you ask Dougal to complete his science homework?

PPPS – please could you ask Dougal to complete his English homework?

PPPPS – If I find out that Dougal had anything to do with your contact details being incorrect, I will have to write another letter about that.

Guess What ?! /

It was me who went into Mum's email and informed the school that their contact details had changed! I did it because I don't want the school to disturb my parents' busy lives by contacting them to rat on me.

I can also tell you that the reason the other letters didn't make it home is because I fed them to the dog. Mr Truss posted the third one, but I managed to snatch it off the postman first and feed it to the dog. But I missed this one.

Now I've been grounded until I've done my ICT project. I don't even know what my ICT project is! I can't do my maths, English and science homework sheets either, because I fed them to the dog and they have already come out the other end.

No way am I doing them now.

AND Dad says I have to clean the car for nothing until he's finished being cross with me, which is very unfair, as he says he's still cross from last time I was grounded. That was because Mr Truss called him while he was up his ladder cleaning Mrs Dogan's windows, to tell him that I'd scrunched up my maths sheets and turned them into a football to kick around the classroom, which is much more fun than maths. It's not my fault my ball landed

right on Mr Truss's
bald head. Dad
had to leave Mrs
Dogan's windows
half done and come
into school to hear
me being falsely
accused of assault.
Mrs Dogan refused
to pay Dad and threatened to find another
window cleaner.

All this means Dad hasn't paid me for
cleaning his car for ages and I have no
money. Even worse, I'm not allowed out until
I've done my ICT project and all my other
homework. My parents don't understand
that by making me stay in my room, they are
being very cruel. That's because my football
team, Fairford United, need me. I should be

at Friday evening training right now, instead of being stuck here. I need to practise my goal keeping skills because we have a very important match on Sunday against our main rivals, Ocklesford Rovers.

Oh no! I've just realised that if I haven't done my project by then, I won't be able to play in Sunday's match!

I could try and escape, but my room is in the loft and it's too far down to jump out of the window. I can't sneak down the stairs because my sister Sibble is in her room, waiting to pounce the moment she sees me, so she can tell Mum and Dad I'm trying to escape.

There's only one thing I can do to escape this terrible situation — I'm going to have to do my ICT project. If only I knew what it was.

I've messaged George, Billy and Burt to find out what the ICT project was. Just to make sure, I messaged Claude as well. Here are their replies:

George

Why weren't you at football training?

18:33

Burt

Why weren't you at football training?

18:34

Billy

We need to discuss tactics for Sunday's match against Ocklesford Rovers.

18:35

Claude

I think I trod in dog poo at training.

18:36

I messaged them all again — in capital letters this time. Here are their replies:

George

You should have been at football training – Billy's dad and Tom had a row. It was awesome!

18:37

Burt

Ask Billy what the ICT project was – his dad should know, he's our teacher!

18:38

Billy

Dad has just reminded me that I should call him Mr Truss at school and not Dad. That way he can cope better if I hang out with you.

18:39

Claude

It wasn't dog poo – it was mud.

18:40

You may or may not have guessed from all this that Tom is our football coach. We play for Fairford United and I am their star goalkeeper. Mr Truss, my teacher, is also my friend Billy's dad.

I tried again. This time I used capital letters and lots of exclamation marks. These are the replies:

George

Tom was cross with Billy's dad because of that letter he wrote to your parents. He said it's not fair you have to miss football because you didn't do his homework. So Billy's dad resigned and Tom needs a new assistant coach.

19:01

Burt

Do you mean the ICT project we finished TWO WEEKS ago? Why do you want to know about that?

19:02

Billy

Please call him Mr Truss, not Billy's dad. The
project was to build a website. It should be
about a hobby, interest or something factual.
I did mine on unusual phenomena.

19:03

Claude

What's a phenomena?

19:04

Billy

It's the plural of phenomenon.

19:05

Me

What's a phenomenon?

19:06

Billy

According to Dad – I mean,
Mr Truss – you are.

19:07

Me

So it's a rare and beautiful thing?

11:27

Billy

Not exactly. A phenomenon is something that occurs without explanation, such as alien abduction, birds flying in formation, lightning striking the same spot twice, or Angela squirting blood from her eyes*.

11:28

*This is NOT Angela Sweeter, who is in my class and wouldn't let me kiss her (it was a dare, I didn't really want to kiss her). Much as I would love to see it, that Angela does not squirt blood from her eyes. But I do have a very interesting (or should I say *phenomenal*?) pet horned lizard called Angela. Horned lizards are thought by some to be the most ugly creatures in the world (not true — my sister Sibble is way more ugly than a horned lizard) and they really do squirt blood from their eyes, but only when they are very worried.

Mr Truss thinks I'm a phenomenon! I have no idea why he's always so cross with me, perhaps it's so the other kids don't get jealous.

And guess what? Tom and Mr Truss had an argument about me! I can imagine how it went:

Tom:

I can't believe it! Our star goalkeeper isn't at training. Something terrible must have happened.

Mr Truss:

Who is your star goalkeeper?

Tom:

Dougal Daley, of course! The best goalkeeper in our league.

Tom's mobile phone rings to the tune of Match of the Day.

Tom (on mobile):

But that's terrible! I will have a word with Mr Truss right away.

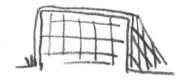

Mr Truss:

You may call me *Billy's dad* while I'm at football training, *Mr Truss* while at school. What terrible thing has happened to Dougal?

Tom (sounding cross):

Dougal has been grounded because you sent his parents a rude and untruthful letter about him. How can you be assistant coach if you keep grounding my best player?

Mr Truss:

In that case, I will have to stop being your assistant coach as we have a clear conflict of interest here. Goodbye. Come on, Billy, we're going home!

Billy:

But training hasn't started yet! Can I go home with Burt?

Burt:

What's a conflict of interest?

Mr Truss:

It means I have enough of being Dougal Daley's teacher, without being assistant coach to his football team as well. I resign! (Stomps off like he does at school when he can't answer one of my questions.)

oh No! WHeRe is Dougie?

NOOO!!!

I wish I'd been there to see it. But, if I'd been there, that would mean I hadn't been grounded and it wouldn't have happened. Now I'm not sure what I wish.

My ICT PROJECT

I have just had a text from Mum:

Please come down for dinner! I have called you several times and it's going cold.

I've texted back:

I can't possibly come down to dinner! I'm far too busy trying to do an ICT project, so I can play in Sunday's match against Ocklesford Rovers. I will gladly sacrifice tonight's brown goo to the dog.

I've just had a text from Dad:

Come down to dinner right now. Mum is very upset because you called her dinner brown goo and Sybil is upset because Eric has dumped her. If you upset anyone now it won't make any difference, so you may as well join us. Or else you will be grounded. for the next match as well.

Why are my parents so mean and unfair?

Mum cooked something different for dinner. Instead of brown goo, we had — wait for it — yellow goo. It looked like sick. Even Sibble didn't eat it. She sat opposite me staring at her plate, instead of eating everything and then saying how delicious it was, just to spite me.

Mum said it was a korma from a fool proof recipe. I can tell you, it wasn't Mum proof. Even the dog wasn't impressed.

'Eat up, Dougie,' said Mum.

'Me?' I said. 'What about Sibble?'

'Leave Sibble alone,' said Dad.

'Why? Has she had a mouthful and is she going to be sick now?' That would be great — I could see if I could tell the difference between Mum's yellow goo and Sibble's sick.

'Shut up!' Sibble screwed up her face so she looked worse than all the horned lizards in the world having an ugly contest. 'Shut up!'

For a moment I thought she really might squirt blood from her eyes — that would be even better than sick. But only tears came out — with an interesting blubbering sound.

'Poor Sibble,' said Mum. She leaned over and gave Sibble a hug, which meant I had to lean over so I could observe the strange faces Sibble was making.

Dad pulled me back.

'Leave your sister alone,' he warned.

'Don't worry, Sibble,' said Mum. 'He wasn't worth it.'

'Who wasn't worth it?' I asked.

'Tell Dougie to shut up!' blubbed Sibble, making a patch of gob on Mum's top.

'Don't worry,' said Mum. 'You'll soon have another boyfriend.'

So that's why she was blubbing — because Eric dumped her! I put on my most helpful face and offered her some brotherly advice. 'You won't get a boyfriend if you look like that.'

'Just shut UP!'
The next thing I
knew, Sibble's
plate of korma
was flying
across the table,
right at my face.

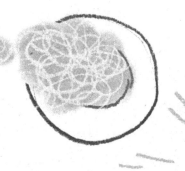

31

Thanks to my skills as a goalie, I managed to punch the plate away, while doing a spectacular dive. My plate went back across the table and landed on Sibble's lap, while I landed on the dog. Sibble ran out, adding an interesting screeching sound to her blubbing, while I played wrestling with the dog and Dad shouted about not understanding why he could never eat his dinner in peace.

None of that helped with the problem of designing a website and completing three lost homework sheets. My friends were no help, so in the end I had to do it myself. This is what I came up with:

Dynamo DD's

PHENOMENAL Services!!

We do anything you want –
absolutely anything

(for a small fee)

HOME

OUR SERVICES

OUR VERY REASONABLE RATES

SATISFIED CUSTOMERS

CONTACT

HOME

Is your **life** in a **mess?**

Are you **far** too **busy** to sort it out?

Contact us!

Our job is to do the jobs you can't – or won't – do

(for a small fee)

Here you will find the answers to all your problems!

OUR SERVICES

Cooking:

Does your ungrateful son always complain about your brown goo? Perhaps he has a point. Let us teach you how to cook meals your children will love, like burgers, chips or pizza.

House cleaning:

Is your house in a right state? Do you rush around tidying and cleaning whenever you have a visitor? Are you always complaining about the mess your children make? Can you never find the TV remote?

If you live in a tip, we will sort you out in no time. Bin liners provided.

Find a job

Are you bored with your work, over-worked and underpaid? Do you come home all tired and grumpy with your children? Would you like to earn more money so you can buy your kids decent takeaways every night?

Let us find your dream job with lots of money.

This is just a small example of what we do. We can also do the following:

- Rescue cats from up trees
- Teach you how to play football
- Find the TV remote
- Make you look pretty for your boyfriend (may be an extra charge, depending on how difficult this is)
- Do your homework for you
- Explain the offside rule

We will do **anything** you want for the very **reasonable** fee of £10

This is what people say about us – honest!

You are brilliant! You are so thoughtful and kind. And clever. And so good at football! Could you help me find the TV remote now?
(Gonan Lostit, Wearsiggon, Berks)

Thank you for trying so hard to make me look pretty for my boyfriend. He still dumped me. Can I have my money back?
(Stella Pain, Uggleton, Middx)

My life hasn't been the same since I found your website! My house is spotless, I've learnt how to cook decent dinners, I have a very easy but well-paid job and my children are happy.
(Mrs Rich, Poshford, Surrey)

Thank you for explaining the offside rule. From now on I will be a better referee.
(Imal Bent, Cheaton, Wick)

I can't believe how reasonable your rates are!
(Gladys Sawyer, Gleeford, Salop)

To contact us, please fill in the form below and press 'send'.

Name:

Address:

e-mail:

Confirm e-mail:

SEND

We will be in touch as soon as we've cleared the back-log of satisfied customers.

How awesome is that? The best ever website or what? I'd say it was PHENOMENAL.

I managed to do it despite Dad coming in, peering over my shoulder and laughing at it until I told him to go away.

Then I messaged George:

Me

Here is my website for the ICT project, so you can look at it and tell me how brilliant it is.

20:00

Sometime later, I messaged him again:

Me

Hurry up, I'm dying to see what you think!

20:20

A bit more time later, I messaged him again:

Me

Are you there, George?

20:22

And again:

Me

George?

20:23

Finally, he replied:

George

Sorry, Dougie, I had to wait for the computer. We only have one, and two of my sisters and three of my step-brothers were in the queue before me. Cool website! Can I help you do some of the jobs and earn some money?

20:50

My reply:

Me

It's not a real website! But you've given me an idea about how to make a bit of money . . .

20:51

His answer:

George

If it's not real, how come it's got a hit counter with 50 hits? Oh, you've been looking at it yourself, of course!
20:52

I copied my website on to a USB stick and was very careful not to let the dog have it.

At school, I handed the USB stick to Mr Truss, who raised his eyebrows, frowned and gave it a very suspicious look. 'Why are you handing me this today?' he asked. 'I said I needed it for Monday and it's only Friday.'

He really ought to learn to be more grateful.

'And where is your maths, English and science homework?' he said.

Some teachers are never happy.

Homework Sheets

When I came home from school, I found Dad playing FIFA. In the unlikely event you don't know what this it, it's a game where you control your own football team and beat your dad's team — it's a great way of making dads angry.

I challenged him to a game. He couldn't resist. As usual, my team, Dynamo DD, beat his, Team Dad. I was still gloating when he folded his arms and gave me a look.

'Aren't you supposed to be grounded?'
He always says that when he loses.

'I've done my ICT project,' I said.
'Despite your interference. Now I can go
to Saturday football training tomorrow
morning and play in Sunday's match.'

'Oh no,' he said. 'You have to do your
maths homework as well.'

I'd hoped he'd forgotten about that.

'And your science homework.'

I'd hoped he'd forgotten about that as well.

'And your English.'

'Fancy another game?' I said, to
distract him. 'So I can prove I didn't beat
you by luck?'

He couldn't resist. I beat him 3-0.

'Right,' he said. 'No football training
until you've done your homework. No
arguing.'

I should have let him win. Now I have to do homework sheets, when I fed them to the dog long ago. I'm going to have to make up my own.

I'll start with my least favourite — maths.

MATHS HOMEWORK SHEET

Topic – problem solving

Level – Good for Geeks

See if you can solve the following problems without falling asleep.

1. If the opposition is coming at you and you think they might score, how far out of the goal should you come?

    a) About three paces

    b) About six paces

    c) Depends how big the opposition is and how brave you are feeling

2. If your dog is fed twice a day, but you have to sneak feed him your dinner, plus the leftover lunch you brought back from school, plus two homework sheets you haven't done and a note from your teacher, how many times was is he really fed?

3. Your dad has lost the TV remote. He couldn't find it yesterday either, nor last Thursday. He lost it eight times last month. What are the chances of him finding it now?

4. Your sister is putting on nail varnish. She has five shades of pukey pink, eight shades of ghastly green, three shades of yucky yellow, a million shades of purple (that's her favourite colour) and twenty shades of boring blue. How much nail varnish does she need to stop herself looking totally ugly?

5. Your teacher keeps giving you homework sheets. You lost two, the dog ate four, you tore three up because they were so boring, you scrunched six up to make a football, because your teacher banned real footballs. How long will it be before your teacher realises he should give you something interesting to do?

Cool, huh? If you ever need a maths homework sheet to replace one you've lost, you can use this one!

I was putting the finishing touches to it, when something awesome and amazing happened. My mobile buzzed with an email – from my website!

To: Dynamo DD >

From: Igor Meerkat >

Dear Dynamo DD,

Please help me because I am desperate. My wife spend all my money, because she think I have good job. I tell her I work in bank and make lots of money, but I am really a window cleaner who earns hardly anything. But now I find your website and see that you will find me good job with lots of money. Give me a job and I will give you £10.
Yours
Igor Meerkat

Someone out there has seen my website and replied! All I have to do is find him a job and I've got £10. I replied immediately:

To: Igor Meerkat >

From: Dynamo DD >

Of course I will find you a job! I will go and look at my long list of people who want someone just like you.

I sent our coach Tom a text:

I've heard you were looking for a new assistant coach to replace Mr Truss. Might I suggest Igor Meerkat? He's very keen and will never give me homework like Mr Truss, so it won't be his fault if I'm grounded.

I replied to Igor Meerkat:

To: Igor Meerkat >

From: Dynamo DD >

Good news! I have found you a job. You will be assistant to the most amazing coach to the best football team in Division One. His name is Tom Spooner and he has brought our club up from the depths to be fourth in Division One. His team are all ace players, especially his goalie. With a bit of help, Tom thinks we could make it into the Premier League.

We train every Friday evening and Saturday mornings on the playing fields off Fairford Road. We will be playing a match there on Sunday. If you turn up and ask for Tom, he will be expecting you.

Please pay your £10 to their goalie, who will pass it on to Dynamo DD.

I'd barely finished, when a text pinged in from Tom:

Igor who?

I'd barely read it, when I had a reply from Igor Meerkat.

To: Dynamo DD >

From: Igor Meerkat >

Thank you, thank you, thank you! My wife is mad on footballers. She say it a pity you only play in Division One but maybe I help you go to Championship then Premiership and play with the great Manchester United.

I come on Sunday! I look forward to you tell me how much money they pay me.

In order to show him just how efficient we are at Dynamo DD, I replied immediately:

To: Igor Meerkat >

From: Dynamo DD >

I don't think we are quite ready to play Manchester United, who are not as great as you think – Stamford United are better. You may talk to Tom about how much he will pay you.

Then I texted Tom:

Your new assistant coach is very keen to start and already has plans to bring us to the West Middlesex Junior Boys Premiership. He says he can make us good enough to play Manchester United.

He will be at the match on Sunday to discuss his contract. Please remind him to pay me my fee.

Tom replied:

What on earth are you talking about?

I've told him I will explain it all at football training tomorrow. I can't wait.

I never made it to football training. That's because, while I was making plans to turn myself into a billionaire boy with a string of cool websites and an army of people working for me (with Mum taking calls and talking in her posh voice, Dad cleaning the office windows and Sibble cleaning the toilets, while I swing around on my big leather chair), I'd forgotten all about my English and science homework sheets. Then my rat of a sister reminded my parents I was still grounded until I'd done them, so instead of football training, I had to make up two more homework sheets.

It's no wonder Eric dumped my sister.

ENGLISH HOMEWORK SHEET

Topic – Spelling and stuff

Level – Good for making you fall asleep

Choose the correct words for the following sentences.

1. Dougal Daley was a clever boy who was always **bored/board** in school. That was **due/dew** to his **teacher/teecher** Mr Truss being the most boring **teecher/teacher** ever.

2. Dougal Daley was a brilliant footballer. He would have **been/bean** even more brilliant if his **mean/mien** and unfair parents didn't ground him all the time because of his rat of a sister, so he had to **Mr/Mrs/Ms** miss training.

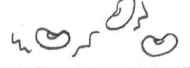

3. Punctuate the following sentences. Are you sure there should be a comma right there? Where DO semi-colons go? Don't forget to put some full stops in so we can breathe!

Some people think that the horned lizard is the most ugly creature on earth but I do not agree with that I can think of lots of things more ugly than horned lizards for example my sister sibble in fact when I put my horned lizard angela next to sibble it is very easy to tell which is the most ugly especially when sibble is screaming or blubbing because her boyfriend dumped her.

Most ugly

SCIENCE HOMEWORK SHEET

Topic: Heat, Sound and Balance

<u>Level</u> – Perfect for Nerds

Try the following experiments and write down what happened.

<u>**Heat**</u>

An oven will keep warm for a long time after you switch it off. This means your mum can put a plate of dinner in the oven after she's switched it off and it will keep warm until you come home from football training. But what happens if she forgot to turn the oven off and it carries on cooking at full blast?

Time until everyone
notices the smell   _____

Time until smoke comes
out of the oven   _____

Time until flames come out
of the oven   _____

Time until everyone
blames you for not coming
home sooner   _____

Appearance of dinner   _____

Your appearance when
you look at your dinner   _____

Sound

Try all these and put them in order, loudest to quietest:

    a. Your sister's scream when you sneak up behind her and go BOO!!!

    b. Your mother's scream when she finds Ida, your pet spider, in the bath.

    c. Your dad's shout when he finds the TV remote in your room.

    d. Your sister's screech after doing the balance experiment below.

Balance

Fill a bucket with water and balance it very carefully on top of an open door.

    a. How far does the door have to open before the bucket falls off?

    b. How wet does your sister get when the bucket falls on her head?

    c. How loud does she screech?

    d. How long will you be grounded

Sunday's Match

I filled in my homework sheets (I got everything right) and waved them in front of Dad while he was reading the paper. Unfortunately, I'd already missed training by then, but I went to the fields in the afternoon with George, Billy, Burt and Claude. Luckily, Claude didn't step on a dog poo, but he did manage to fall over in the only muddy puddle on the whole field.

Everything was going fine until Sunday's match.

Dad told me he'd be along at the start of the match, then didn't turn up — in fact, I prefer it, because then I don't have to listen to him shouting instructions at me while I pretend he's not my dad. But if I'd known he wasn't going to turn up, I wouldn't have had to spend half the match looking out for him, to make sure he hadn't brought the dog with him.

Our dog thinks he's our star player— he doesn't understand that a typical football team only has eleven players. He doesn't appreciate that you can't trip everyone up whether they are in your team or not. He doesn't understand that you are not supposed to attack the ball. He doesn't know that chasing the ball into the goal I'm defending is not clever and neither is standing there wagging his tail with a deflated ball in his mouth while the opposition leap about because the dog scored them a goal.

But Dad didn't turn up at the start, so all my worrying was in vain. I spent the rest of the time looking out for Igor Meerkat. He didn't turn up either. But, while I was scanning the crowd of parents for him, three balls went past me and into my goal.

But the other three weren't my fault! They were Burt's dad fault. He was linesman and kept looking over to the edge of the field, where a strange figure in a long dark coat and big furry hat was

standing with his hands in his pockets watching us. That meant Burt's dad didn't raise his flag for offside and Ocklesford Rovers scored three goals they shouldn't have. They were SO offside!

At half-time, Tom went over to talk to the strange man, but he ran away.

Dad turned up at the end of the match. Tom asked him if he'd like to be assistant coach. It didn't matter what I said, Dad refused to give me £10 for getting him the job.

I went home in a very bad mood. Then I had an email from Igor Meerkat:

To: Dynamo DD >

From: Igor Meerkat >

I come and watch you play today and I can't believe it! You are mad if you think this team is ever going to play Manchester United! Then the coach came over and I ran away before he ask me to be assistant coach. Then I fall in the river. You make me a lot of trouble and now I want you give me a job and I pay you nothing for it.

From Me – Igor Meerkat.

The man in the big coat and furry hat was Igor Meerkat? Well, he didn't look like much of a football coach anyway, so here is my reply:

To: Igor Meerkat >

From: Dynamo DD >

Dear Mr Meerkat, I didn't realise that was you lurking around today. You should have come closer to see how brilliant we are. But we now have a new coach, who is going to fit us in with his busy window cleaning job.

I'd just sent it when another email came in.

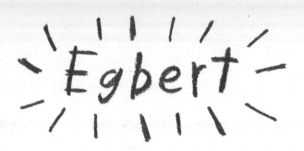

To: Dynamo DD >

From: Egbert Truss >

Dear Dynamo DD,

Please help me. I am a very busy teacher and you wouldn't believe how much time I spend marking piles of homework sheets. And still the kids complain because they have to do them! After a hard day at school, I would like to come home to a clean house. Even though I have just resigned as assistant coach to a local football team, I don't have time to clean the house myself. Please could you find someone to clean my house for me? I will pay £8.00 per hour for ten hours of cleaning and give you £10 for finding the right person. If you can find someone for me tomorrow (Monday) I will pay you double. That's 2 x £10 = £20.

Yours in anticipation

Egbert Truss

An email from my teacher! From Billy's dad! AND his name is Egbert! No wonder Billy won't tell us what his dad's name is.

He must have seen my phenomenal website and been so impressed he had to contact me for help. Tomorrow at school, I expect him to apologise for doubting me before telling me how my ICT project is the best ever and well worth waiting for. He might even tell everyone how brilliant I am.

I have just the person for his cleaning job – Igor Meerkat. I sent him an email.

To: Igor Meerkat >

From: Dynamo DD >

_____

Dear Mr Meerkat, I have found you another job. You will clean a teacher's house for £800 per hour, for ten hours. If you do it tomorrow (Monday), I will give you a bonus of £5.

He replied straight away:

To: Dynamo DD >

From: Igor Meerkat >

Yes I will do this! I borrow my mother's very best feather duster to do the job nice! No need to give me £5 bonus when he gives me all that money for cleaning it.

I sent an email to Mr Truss:

To: Egbert Truss >

From: Dynamo DD >

Dear Egbert,
I have found someone to clean your house for you. He is very happy with your fee and will do it tomorrow (Monday). If you would like some help on how to make your lessons more interesting, I could supply you with exciting home-work sheets for £10 each.

I've had another request! Here it is:

To: Dynamo DD >

From: Elwitz Sanderly >

This is the job. You will give me a secure address for delivery of an envelope. You will receive the envelope. You will wait until someone else comes to collect it. You will receive £10 per envelope. You will TELL NO ONE about it.

How easy is that? All I have to do is give Mr Sanderly an address where he can deliver an envelope. I know just the person.

Me

Claude, how would you like to earn some money? All you have to do is stay in and wait for an envelope. Then you have to wait until the envelope is collected by someone else. Easy! I will pay you £100 per envelope. Just give me your address.

23:01

He messaged me back almost straight away:

Claude

You're going to pay me one hundred pounds for looking after envelopes? Yes please! You know my address, it's round the corner from Billy.

23:01

I messaged back:

Me

I am going to pay you ONE pound per envelope. I know you live round the corner from Billy, but what is your actual address?

23:02

Claude replied:

Claude

I checked your email and you definitely said £100. I think you forgot to put the little dot in. It doesn't matter though, I am happy to have £1.00. Or £1. My address is 1 Dipp Street, Ocklesford, Middx. Middx is short for Middlesex.

23:03

My reply:

Me

Little dots? You sound as bad as Mr Truss! I will tell you when to expect your first envelope. And I KNOW what Middx stands for.

23:04

I emailed Mr Sanderly right away:

To: Elwitz Sanderly >

From: Dynamo DD >

___

I have a secret address for delivery of envelope. It is 1 Dipp Street, Ocklesford, Middx. Middx is short for Middlesex. Could I have a pound coin in my payment?

His reply:

To: Dynamo DD >

From: Elwitz Sanderly >

___

I KNOW what Middx is short for! You will be paid a single £10 note, no arguing. Await instructions.

I messaged Claude:

Me

I will pay you a single £10 after ten envelopes.

00:00

An email came in from Mr Truss:

To: Dynamo DD >

From: Egbert Truss >

_____

Thank you for your offer to provide me with homework
sheets. I'm afraid our school budget will not run to the cost
of these, but we do have a good supply. I look
forward to having my house cleaned tomorrow (Monday).
I would like it done while I am at school. I will leave a key
under the geranium.

I don't know what a geranium is, but I
emailed Mr Meerkat right away:

To: Dynamo DD >

From: Mr Meerkat >

_____

Please clean teacher's house tomorrow during school hours. You will find the key under the geranium.

He didn't reply, so I guess he knows what a geranium is.

DOG POO and Claude's Shoe

This morning I walked to school with a big grin on my face, even though it's Monday. Until I met the others — who were talking about yesterday's match.

'We need to make sure that Dougie doesn't let any goals in,' said George.

'It's not my fault!' I said. 'I need a decent defence!'

'What's wrong with your defence?' said Burt. Burt is our defender. He's so big the opposition find it hard to get past him. But sometimes they do. Especially if they trip him up and the cheating referee says it wasn't a foul.

'OK,' I said. 'We just have to make sure we score more goals.'

'I do my best!' said George. He's our ace winger and top scorer. 'But sometimes there are just too many goals let in the other end.' He looked at me.

'It's not my fault!' I said. 'I need a decent defence!'

'You said that already,' said Burt. 'What's wrong with your defence?'

'Dog poo,' said Claude. Claude plays in mid-field. He runs around aimlessly and the opposition don't know what he's doing either.

Burt stepped in front of Claude, made himself look even bigger and glared down at him. 'Are you saying my defence is dog poo?'

'It's all over my shoe,' said Claude. 'Can you help me wipe it off?'

'No way!' We ran off, while Claude danced around scraping his shoe over the grass.

When Claude caught us up, he was only wearing one shoe. 'I had to take the other one off to wash it in the river,' he said. He meant the River Ockle. It runs along the fields where we play football and we walk along it on the way to and from school. I don't know why it's called a river– it's barely a trickle.

'My shoe was washed away in the current,' said Claude.

Only Claude could have managed that in a river that has no current.

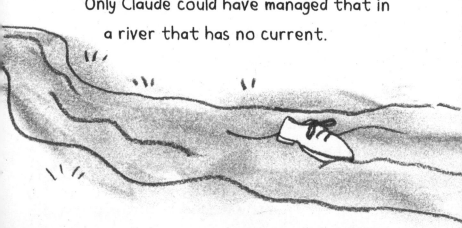

At school I waited for Mr Truss to say something about my website, but he didn't. By lunchtime, I decided I would have to ask him.

'What did you think of my awesome phenomenal website?' I said.

'You'll find out soon enough,' he said. 'Go and have your lunch.'

I ate lunch and went into the playground with George, Burt, Billy and Claude to play football without a ball (we're not allowed footballs in the playground – health and safety). I was about to make a spectacular save, when I saw something odd. Mr Truss was on his bike, cycling away from school.

'Where's Billy's dad going?' I asked George, who was about to score the spectacular goal that I would save spectacularly.

'Hey, that's cheating!' he said. 'Trying to put me off when I'm about to score.'

'Don't call him *my dad*,' said Billy. 'He's *Mr Truss* at school.'

'Do you think my shoe would have reached the sea by now?' said Claude.

I found out later what Mr Truss was up to.

Aprons and Dusters

Before I tell you where Mr Truss was
sneaking off to at lunchtime, I must tell you
what happened as we arrived outside Billy's
house after school. We'd gone there to
discuss tactics.

'Someone's in Billy's house!' said Claude.
We all stopped. Someone was in Billy's living-
room, wearing a flowery apron, a silly hat
and waving a feather duster.

'Hide!' I said, dipping behind the front
garden wall.

We all ducked. Burt popped up to have
a better look. 'It's the mad man from the
football match. The one who ran off when
Dad went over to have a word with him.'

'What's he doing in my house?' said Billy.

'He's cleaning it,' I said. 'Because your dad's too busy thinking up boring lesson plans.'

'How do you know?' said Billy.

Before I could answer, we heard Billy's front door open and close. Then we heard footsteps coming down the path, the gate squeaked open, banged shut and the footsteps went away down the road. Just before he went round the corner, I caught a glimpse of his big coat, furry hat and the feather duster he carried over his shoulder.

'Who *is* that?' said Burt.

'That's Igor,' I said. 'He came to clean Billy's house because he couldn't make us as good as Manchester United.'

They all looked at me as though I'd just let six goals in. So I told them how I was going to earn £20 for making Igor clean Billy's house. When I'd finished, they looked at me like I'd just saved six penalties at the same time.

As soon as I was home, Mum came rushing out of the kitchen, waving a letter at me. That's when I found out why Mr Truss had sneaked off on his bicycle during lunch-break today. Instead of sending his latest letter home for me to feed to the dog, he'd gone to the estate agent where Mum works and delivered it to her — how sneaky is that?

OCKLESFORD JUNIOR SCHOOL

Duty Road, Ocklesford, Middx

Dear Mr and Mrs Daley

I am very sorry to be writing to you so soon after my last letter, but I must inform you that your son DOUGAL DALEY has not completed his ICT project.

What he handed me is clearly a copy of a website that he has downloaded onto his USB stick. I had my suspicions when he gave it to me on Friday instead of today (Monday). That's a whole weekend before I asked for it and Dougal NEVER completes his tasks on time. The website Dynamo DD's PHENOMENAL Services is far too good for the skills that Dougal sadly lacks. I doubt whether he even knows what *phenomenal* means.

In order to test my suspicions, I have made use of the website, to prove that Dynamo DD's Phenomenal Services is real. They have arranged for someone to clean my house. If you ever need someone to clean your house, I can recommend their services.

Please keep Dougal grounded until he has completed his ICT project to my satisfaction.

Yours sincerely
Mr E Truss

That's the last time I'm going to make an effort with anything I do for Mr Truss!

Unfortunately, Mum had come home in a bad mood because of work. She's an estate agent and her boss has given her next door's house to sell. That's where the crook Lysander Witzel used to live with his son Stan, but it has been empty since they moved out when I rumbled their crooky activities in a previous book.

I tried to tell her that Mr Truss was wrong, but she still grounded me. She didn't even wait for Dad.

'But Dad can prove it was my own website!' I protested. 'He saw it himself!'

Mum gave me her *I don't believe you* look. Luckily, Dad came home soon after.

'You'll never guess what Dougal's done now,' said Mum, waving Mr Truss's letter at him.

'It's not my fault!' I said. 'Mr Truss thinks that I cheated and someone else did my website for me — tell Mum it's not true!'

Dad read the letter. 'Er, sorry, Dougie, I can't do that,' he said. 'I don't want to get into trouble with Mr Truss for helping you.'

'But you didn't!' I protested. 'All you did was laugh!'

'But you keep telling me Mr Truss doesn't believe anything,' said Dad. 'Tell you what — do another website and I'll forget about the last car clean you owe me.'

That was tempting, but not enough. 'All car cleans,' I said. 'And I get paid for the next one.'

Dad thought for a while. 'Deal,' he said.

I now have to think up another website, but I suppose that's better than cleaning the car without pay.

I set up a chat with George, Burt, Billy and Claude for ideas. Here are their responses:

George

Can you find me a job?

17:30

Burt

Can you find me a job?

17:31

Billy

Can you find me a job?

17:32

Claude

Could your dog find my shoe?

17:33

I have no choice. I'll have to design my own website. Again.

My ICT Project Again!

HOME

Interesting Maths

Interesting English

Interesting Science

Interesting Homework

THE MAKING SCHOOL INTERESTING WEBSITE

boring

● **HOME**

Are you the most boring teacher in the world?

Look at this website and make school more fun

for your poor kids!

INTERESTING MATHS

Think this is impossible? It is. But the answer is easy – just don't do any maths and school will already become more interesting!

INTERESTING ENGLISH

Read a book with a brilliant battle scene and then ask your kids to act it out in the playground, using plastic swords (health and safety). Have one class fight the other. The winning class gets a day off school.

HOME

Interesting
Maths

Interesting
English

Interesting
Science

Interesting
Homework

INTERESTING SCIENCE

You can make science interesting by bringing in live maggots.

INTERESTING HOMEWORK

With lessons as interesting as these, who needs homework?

Just as I finished making up another website, I heard the ping of an email. It was from Mr Meerkat.

To: Dynamo DD >

From: Igor Meerkat >

I finish clean the house. Ten hours at £800 per hour is £8,000, please pay me in cash. By the way, I saw some funny looking boys hiding behind the wall when I came out. From Igor.

I sent an email to Mr Truss

To: Egbert Truss >

From: Dynamo DD >

Your house has now been cleaned. Please pay £8,000 in cash plus £20 for my fee.

Here is his reply:

To: Igor Meerkat >

From: Dynamo DD >

Following your email, I should remind you that we agreed that I would pay £8.00 per hour for ten hours work. That would be £80 altogether, not £8,000. I think you forgot the little dot when you promised to pay the cleaner £800 per hour.

I should also inform you that my house was not cleaned very well. I left for school at 8.00am and returned at 4.30pm. My son returned at 3.30pm with some friends and said they saw a strange man leaving the house with a feather duster over his shoulder. Therefore, the cleaner was only there for seven and a half hours at the most. Also, the house was still in a terrible state when I returned. I know that my son's friends can be very messy (one of them in particular) but I don't think they would have made that much mess in one hour. My son said they were discussing football tactics and I believe him.

I will therefore not pay anything until my house is properly cleaned.

I sent an email to Igor:

To: Igor Meerkat >

From: Dynamo DD >

The amount for cleaning the teacher's house was £8.00 per hour, not £800! I think you missed the little dot. And you were not there for ten hours. There are witnesses to prove this.

This was his reply:

To: Dynamo DD >

From: Igor Meerkat >

I do clean the house properly and who was it spying on me? I not going back there – if you want it clean, clean it yourself!

That looks like the end of Igor Meerkat. Just as well, as I'm beginning to think there is something weird about him. And it's just as well I have a brilliant plan to find a new cleaner.

To: Elwitz Sanderly >

From: Dynamo DD >

Do you know a good cleaner? I will give you £5 if you find one – it is for a teacher's house, it has to be done while he's out and he leaves the key under the geranium. Pay is £8.00 per hour (to avoid confusion, please note the location of the little dot).

He replied straight away:

To: Dynamo DD >

From: Elwitz Sanderly >

First envelope will be delivered tomorrow at 2.00pm. It will be collected at 2.30pm. Give me the address of the teacher with the geranium and I will see that his house is cleaned – as long as he leaves cash.

I messaged Claude straight away:

Me

Your first envelope arrives at 2.00pm tomorrow. It will be picked up at 2.30pm. Make sure you are in.

22:30

Now to wait for the money to start rolling in!

SCHOOL TRIP

OCKLESFORD JUNIOR SCHOOL

Duty Road, Ocklesford, Middx

Dear Parent/Guardian,

OCKLESFORD JUNIOR SCHOOL TRIP TO MORDEN MANOR

This trip is an important part of your son/daughter's education. It will cover topics including maths, science, English, history, geography, art, music and some other things. Morden Manor is a large country house set in many acres of grounds. It has several classrooms, where the children can see what school was like long ago. It has a mini-beast trail*, adventure playground*, art gallery, ICT lab, picnic area, small zoo*, large insect collection*, plus many other exciting activities.

The coach will leave school on Friday at 8.30am PROMPT. Please make sure your child is on time!

Please sign the consent form below and send it in with £10.00 to cover the cost of the trip.

E Truss
Teacher

*Due to health and safety regulations, we won't be doing any of this.

Consent Form

Name of Child:

....

I consent to my son/daughter going on the trip to

Morden Manor

I enclose £10 towards the cost of the trip

Signed .... Parent/guardian

'Dougal?' said Mum. It was dinner time and she had that knowing look on her face. The one where she sort of raises her eyebrows, tips her head down until she gets a double chin and then looks up at me. 'Why are you being so quiet?'

I couldn't believe it. Normally she complains because I make too much noise. 'I'm thinking,' I said. Which was true. I was thinking about all the money I was going to make with my secret website. I was thinking about buying a private jet, so I could nip over to New York and see how George was getting on as Chief Executive of the US Division of Dynamo DD Phenomenal Enterprises.

'Thinking?' said Dad. 'That makes a change. What about?'

'About the school trip. Could I have £10 for it?'

Dad sighed. 'What have you done to deserve £10 for the school trip?' He always says that.

'I've done all my homework and two websites because Mr Truss didn't believe my other one was all my own work.'

'OK,' said Dad. 'When you've cleaned my car, you can use the £10 I give you for the school trip.'

'That is so unfair!' I said. 'This trip is an important part of my education. It says so in the letter.'

'Let's see the letter then,' said Mum.

'Good idea,' said Dad. 'Then we can make sure the trip is real.'

That was a problem. I couldn't find the letter. 'Of course it's real!' I said.

'The last one wasn't,' said Sibble. 'You just asked for the money and then spent it on maggots.'

'Those maggots were an important part of my education,' I said. 'I was conducting a scientific experiment.'

'To see how fast you could fill the house with flies,' said Sibble. 'Gross.'

'No, it was to watch your face when I put one down your neck. It was almost as good as your blubbing face.'

This time I did my spectacular dive before she'd picked her plate up to throw at me. Unfortunately, I managed to knock my own plate off the table at the same time. The dog thought it was great because he could have all my dinner in one go instead of waiting for me to feed it to him a piece at a time.

Mum shouted at me for dropping her dinner and Dad shouted at the dog for eating it. Sibble shrieked with laughter because she'd made me fall off my chair by reaching for her plate without any intention of throwing it.

And then they were all shouting at me for trying to rescue my dinner from the dog's mouth. I managed to rescue three pieces. I put them back on my plate and offered to eat them.

'It's all right, Dougie,' said Mum. 'You don't to have to eat that now. It doesn't look very nice.'

I didn't have the heart to tell her that it looked better after it came out of the dog's mouth than it had before it went in.

'And, while everyone's being quiet for a second,' said Mum. 'Has anyone seen the key to the Witzel house? I'll be in big trouble at work if I've lost it, but it doesn't seem to be in my handbag.'

'That's because you have several handbags,' said Dad. 'And they're all as messy as Dougal's bedroom.'

'What do you mean, quiet for a change?' I said at the same time.

We then had an argument about how messy Mum's handbags are and how noisy dinner time is. It was a very noisy argument. And at the end of it, no one knew where the key to the Witzel house was and I still didn't have my £10 for the school trip.

There was only one thing for it – I would have to ask Mr Truss for another letter about the school trip.

School Trip
– part 2

This morning I asked Mr Truss for a new letter about the trip as soon as we were in the classroom.

'You've lost it already?' he said. 'I only gave them out yesterday! Are you sure your dog hasn't eaten it?'

'I haven't looked in the dog yet,' I said. 'Can I have another one anyway?'

With a big sigh, he opened his folder and took out a letter. 'It's the last one – make sure you don't lose it.'

'I won't – or Dad will refuse to give me the money and I'll have to stay behind while you go on the trip without me.'

For a moment I thought he was going

to change his mind and not give me the letter, but he muttered something about wishful thinking and handed it over.

I spent the rest of the morning until break designing a care home for retired teachers. That's because I've decided that when I've made my millions, I should give some of it to charity. What better cause than a home where teachers can go when they've finished teaching? Here they can live out their lives in classrooms specially adapted for old people, where they can spend all day teaching each other and filling in worksheets. I think they will all be very happy there and it means you will never have to worry about bumping into your old teacher when you grow up.

As Sibble likes her teachers so much, I might employ her as a live-in helper.

'Why is Dougal being so quiet?'

I was interrupted by Angela, talking about me to her friends Jaz and Mia. That's because I don't sit at a table with George and Burt after Mr Truss split us up for being too noisy. Now I have to sit with the girls because Mr Truss thinks they will be good for me, but all they do is giggle or complain.

'Be quiet, I'm thinking!' I said.

Angela giggled. 'Thinking? I've never known you do that before.'

Mia and Jaz giggled as well.

'Stop giggling!' I said. 'I can't concentrate now!'

'Dougal Daley!' said Mr Truss. 'Stop being a nuisance and do your worksheet.'

'I'm not being a nuisance!' I protested. 'I'm thinking!'

'Well, that's a first,' said Mr Truss. 'I don't suppose you know why Claude hasn't come to school today?'

I did my best innocent shrug — I didn't tell him that Claude was staying at home to await delivery of an envelope. I don't want him to know about my website business — I'm going to surprise him one day when he's in the home for old teachers. They will all be sitting in assembly waiting for a VIP visitor — the person who paid for their home. I can't wait to see his face when I walk in.

'I wonder why Claude didn't come to school today,' said Billy, on the way home.

'Maybe he's caught a terrible disease,' said Burt.

'Why don't we go past his house and ask him?' said George.

We went to Claude's house. When he answered the door, he had a £10 note in his hand. 'Here you are, Dougie.'

'Why weren't you in school?' asked Billy.

'I had to stay in for the envelope,' he said. 'It was delivered at 2.00pm, with £10 for Dougie. It was collected at 2.29pm, one minute early. Can I have my pound now?'

I put the £10 in my pocket. 'I told you, I'll pay you £10 when you've done ten envelopes.'

'Why did Claude just give you £10?' asked Burt.

'I'm employing him,' I said. I explained about the envelopes.

'That's not fair,' said Billy. 'You should give Claude at least £5 per envelope.'

'Can I do the next envelope?' asked Burt. 'I'll do it for £3.'

'I'll do it for £2!' said George.

'I'll do it for a pound,' said Claude.

'Done!' I said. 'Now, I must go home and feed Angela some ants.'

'Can I come and watch?' said Claude, George and Billy.

'Can I see her squirt blood out of her eyes?' said Burt, even though he knows horned lizards only do that when upset or frightened.

'I'm not going to upset or frighten Angela so you can see her squirt blood out of her eyes.'

'She'll get upset when Burt looks at her anyway,' said George.

'Not if I smile at her.' Burt gave a smile that would be enough to frighten anybody.

At home, Mum was in the kitchen talking to Mrs Grim. Mrs Grim's our neighbour and she doesn't like me, so I decided to sneak upstairs before she saw me and started asking awkward questions. It's hard to sneak four boys upstairs, especially when one of them is Burt. As we went up, I heard Mrs Grim say something to Mum.

'Did I tell you I saw a great big box being delivered to the Witzel house? Is that Dougal sneaking upstairs? Sounds like there's a herd of elephants with him.'

We ran the rest of the way up.

Having five of us in my room is a squash, especially when Claude tangles himself up in my football kit and falls over. It's just as well Angela is an old horned lizard and used to noise.

Next to Angela's tank is a plastic box, full of big, red, poisonous ants. But the thing about the plastic box is that it's too slippery for the ants to climb up, so they just run about on the bottom of the box on all the leaves and stuff I put in there for them. I like my ants to be nice and happy before Angela eats them. I think they taste better that way.

Feeding Angela is tricky. First you have to coax the ants out of their box and into her tank. You can't let them crawl over you because they bite, and their bites are

nasty. So, I have a pair of special
gloves and a long, flat stick. Once
I've got some ants to climb the
stick, I tap them into Angela's
cage. Then she wanders around
eating them. When she's
finished, I give her some
more, until she's had
enough.

'Cool,' said George.
'She just vacuums them up.'

'Horned lizards use their sticky tongues
to pick up ants,' said Billy. 'But it's so fast
you can't see it.'

'Can I feed her some ants?' asked
George, followed by Burt, Billy and Claude.

I gave George the stick and the glove
and we all watched him put some ants into
Angela's cage. Then Burt had a go and then

Billy. Then Claude had a go. When I say had a go, I mean he put the stick in the box of ants and dropped it. Then he put his hand in the box to grab the stick. Luckily, I stopped him just in time. You really don't want those ants crawling up your arm.

'Do you think we'll see anything like this on our trip to Morden Manor?' said George.

'I don't think we'd be allowed to,' said Billy. 'Health and safety.'

'They won't have anything as cool as Angela,' I said.

'They probably won't even have poisonous ants,' said Burt.

'What trip?' said Claude.

'The one in the letter,' said George. 'It has to be in by tomorrow with the money, or we can't go.'

'Just as well I got the last letter,' I said.

'But what about Claude?' said Billy, Burt and George.

'OK, you can have mine,' I said to Claude. 'I'll make one for me.'

SCHOOL TRIP
- part 3

As soon as they'd gone, I checked my email.

To: Dynamo DD >

From: Elwitz Sanderly >

Today's delivery was successful. Tomorrow there will be two deliveries. One at 10.00am, to be collected at 10.30am. The second at 2.00pm, to be collected at 2.30pm. £10 per envelope.

I messaged Claude straight away.

Me

Two envelopes tomorrow! That's £10 each!

17:15

Then I made a copy of the letter about the school trip.

OCKLESFORD JUNIOR SCHOOL

Duty Road, Ocklesford, Middx

Dear Parent/Guardian

We are very pleased to tell you that we have arranged a special trip to Morden Manor, where your child will receive an amazing education for one day only. But not on all the interesting stuff, because Health and Safety have said that it's not healthy or safe. But we expect some boys will probably sneak off and do those things anyway.

Please fill out slip below and let us take your son/ daughter out for a great day!

Tear-off slip (to be torn off, if you can't find the scissors)

. . . .

I hereby agree that my son/daughter can come on the trip to Morden Manor. Please let him/her go on all the things that Health and Safety say he/she can't.

Name of Child:

. . . .

Signed . . . . Parent/guardian

I've agreed to pay £10 towards the cost and here it is.

. . . .

Today Claude didn't come to school.
I didn't tell Mr Truss it was because he
had to stay in and wait for envelopes.
But I think I might have to forge a letter
explaining why he's not at school.

My forged letter about
the school trip worked,
although Mr Truss did
frown at it for a
while.

Unfortunately,
I had to use my own
money, because my
mean and unfair
parents wouldn't
give me the £10.

This is how the
argument (I mean discussion) went:

Mum (stirring her brown goo):

I've had the most horrible day. It
didn't help that I was already tired
because I couldn't sleep last night. I
kept hearing the strangest noises.

Me:

That would have been Dad snoring.

Dad (from behind his newspaper):

What did you say?

Mum:

No, for once it was something else.
Strange noises coming from next door,
keeping me awake. Then I had a horrible
day.

Dad (putting his newspaper down):

Me too. I was up my ladder, busy cleaning a window, when this mad woman came by demanding money. She made me drop my bucket. Luckily, it didn't land on her.

Mum:

That was me and I wasn't mad. Well, not until you dropped a bucket of dirty water all over me. I needed the money to have another key cut for the Witzel house, as I can't find the last one. I think it might be in the dog. I've been watching him very carefully and I haven't seen it come out yet.

Sibble (in her squeaky girly voice):

Gross!

Dad:

Well I nearly fell off my ladder when you came by and demanded my last £10.

Mum (slopping brown goo all over our plates):

And then when I went to pay for the key, it turned out that the £10 note was a forgery! I've never been more embarrassed in my life. Next time, please give me a proper £10 note.

Me:

Could I have something in my sandwiches other than brown goo? I have enough brown goo at dinner.

Dad:

Don't be rude about your mother's brown
g- - I mean dinner.

Mum:

You had cheese and pickle in your
sandwiches today. But without the cheese
- we've run out.

Me (with a sigh):

Can I have £10 for the school trip?
I've found the letter now.

Mum:

I don't have £10. I gave it to the man
in the key shop and he cut it in half
because it was forged.

Dad:

I can't give you £10 because I gave my last one to your mother.

Mum:

And it was forged, so I still have no key for next door. What happens if someone wants to look at it?

Sibble (waving her hands to dry her nail varnish):

They've had a lucky escape – from living next door to Dougie.

Me:

Or death by nail varnish fumes.

Sibble (waving her hands in front of me):

Die, brother, die!

Me:

Get your stinking hands off me!

Mum (banging our plates onto the table):

Will you two stop arguing and eat your
dinner?

Me:

I'd rather argue. Even with Sibble.

Dad:

Will you stop being so rude about your
mother's dinners?

Me:

OK. If you give me £10 for my school
trip.

Dad:

No way am I giving £10 until you stop being so ungrateful. I haven't got £10 anyway. I gave it to your mother.

Mum:

It was forged.

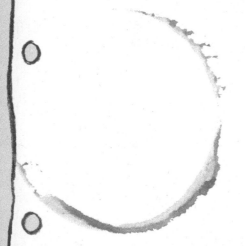

RED DOTS

I've just messaged Claude:

> **Me**
>
> We're going to be rich! Now draw red dots all over your arm.
>
> 07:30

The reason I sent it is because I've had another email from Mr Sanderly, who now wants FOUR envelopes collecting! It means Claude will have to stay off school, but that's not a problem as I can write a note for him. I'm beginning to wonder if I could leave school now and set up my website empire right away.

If you're wondering why I asked Claude to draw red dots all over his arm, you'll have to wait and see. An email has just come in from Mr Truss.

To: Dynamo DD >

From: Mr Truss >

Igor has been back to clean my house. It looks no different. I only know he's been because he took his money, but he left a padded envelope behind. Please ask him to make sure he remembers to take it with him next time. And tell him that if the house isn't cleaned properly, that will be the last time.

That was puzzling. I thought Igor Meerkat had quit. Or maybe this was the cleaner that Mr Sanderly knew. I sent a couple of emails to find out.

To: Elwitz Sanderly >

From: Dynamo DD >

Mr Truss says you have to keep coming back to clean his house until it is done to his satisfaction and please don't leave padded envelopes lying around.

To: Elwitz Sanderly >

From: Dynamo DD >

Did you find someone to clean Mr Truss's house? Did they leave an envelope behind?

I had the following replies:

To: Dynamo DD >

From: Igor Meerkat >

I don't leave anything behind at the teacher's house!

To: Dynamo DD >

From: Elwitz Sanderly >

No envelope was ever left at Mr Truss's house. Say no more on the matter.

Very odd. I think I'll say no more.

1 Dipp Street
Ocklesford
Middx
(Short for Middlesex)

Dear Mr Egbert Truss,

I am very sorry that Claude can't come to school. He has ant bites all over him, from when he went to Dougie's house. You really don't want to let those ants crawl up your arm.

Here is £10 for the school trip to Morden Manor. As long as the ant bites have gone down he will be able to go. Please don't let him do anything that's not healthy or safe.

Yours sincerely,
Bianca Barleycorn
(Claude's Mum)

Now you know why I asked Claude to draw red dots all over his arm. They look just like ant bites!

Forged Notes

OCKLESFORD JUNIOR SCHOOL

Duty Road, Ocklesford, Middx

Dear Parent/Guardian

I am writing to inform you that we have had to take the unfortunate step of cancelling the school trip to Morden Manor. We will be taking an interesting trip to the High Street instead.

This is due to the fact that several of the £10 notes sent in to pay for the trip were sent back to us because they were forged. This is very embarrassing for the school.

In future, please be very careful about the money you send in.

Yours sincerely

E Truss
Teacher

OCKLESFORD GAZETTE

BEWARE OF FORGED £10 NOTES

POLICE HAVE WARNED THE RESIDENTS OF OCKLESFORD not TO USE £10 NOTES, AFTER SEVERAL FORGED BANKNOTES HAVE BEEN USED IN SHOPS. The FORGERIES are Extremely GOOD, but, IF you LOOK at THEM Under a MICROSCOPE, it is POSSIBLE TO SEE THE words 'MADE IN ALBANIA' JUST UNDER THE QUEEN'S HEAD.

MADE IN ALBANIA

'It's very BAD FOR Business', said MR BISCUIT, OWNER OF OCKLESFORD Pet SHOP. 'I'VE LOST £50 From FORGED BANKNOTES.'
AS YET, the POLICE don't KNOW WHERE THE FORGERIES COME FROM. 'PEOPLE DON't REMEMBER WHERE They Obtained These BANKNOTES', said Sergeant DARAMY OF OCKLESFORD POLICE STATION. 'EVEN when they'VE BEEN GIVEN in CHANGE. WE SUGGEST THAT PEOPLE Avoid Using £10 NOTES UNTIL WE GET to the BOTTOM OF THE MATTER.'

I can't believe it! Just when I start earning some money at last, I can't use it, because it's all in £10 banknotes and some of them might be forged.

But luckily, due to my amazing envelope skills, I received the following email from Mr Sanderly:

To: Dynamo DD >

From: Elwitz Sanderly >

_____

You are doing so well, I am going to pay you £20 per envelope.

I messaged Claude:

Me

As we can no longer trust our £10 notes, I will pay you £20 when you have done 20 envelopes.

16:01

By the time we went on the school trip to the High Street (instead of Morden Manor), I had three £20 notes to spend.

Mr Truss made us wear bright orange bibs for the school trip, so we could be seen. The parent helpers had to wear them and Mr Truss wore one as well. I decided I'd rather not be seen than look like a dork. That's why I took mine off as soon as we were in the High Street. It was great. Without the bib, I didn't look like part of the trip, so I could sneak into shops and buy things. This is what I bought.

A cave for Angela's cage and a small box of maggots from Ocklesford Pet Shop.

Some goalie gloves and
a new football from
Speedy Sports.

Twenty assorted
chocolate bars and ten
packets of crisps from
Nippy News.

All the shops had notices on them:

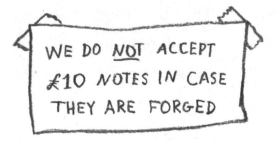

WE DO NOT ACCEPT
£10 NOTES IN CASE
THEY ARE FORGED

That was fine by me, because I only had
£20 notes. I insisted on having all my change
in coins, to make sure that I wasn't given
any forged banknotes. I was just stuffing my

£1.68 change, chocolate bars and crisps into the bag from Speedy Sports, when guess who walked into Nippy News? None other than the Ocklesford Rovers football cheat and son of the crook Lysander Witzel, Stan.

'You were rubbish in goal when we played you, weren't you?' he said.

'Well, it wasn't your skills that helped you score,' I replied. 'But your dad the cheating referee.' As I stood there, I thought there was something not quite right about him.

'So you admit it you're rubbish in goal,' said Stan.

'I admit that I haven't found a good way to deal with cheats,' I said. 'But I will.'

I could still hear him laughing when I left the shop. I don't like Stan Witzel. I can't believe he used to be my friend.

When I came out, I thought I'd lost my class, but I soon spotted the bright orange bibs. I put mine back on while I was sneaking back to join them. That's when I realised what was odd about Stan Witzel. He was wearing jeans and a hoodie. Why wasn't he wearing a school uniform?

'Where have you been?' said Burt.

'Nowhere,' I said.

'You've been sneaking into shops and buying things,' said George, looking at my Speedy Sports carrier bag.

'I don't know why you bothered to take your bib off before you sneaked away,' said Angela. 'You could tell you were sneaking by the way you were walking.'

'Yeah,' said Mia, doing a silly walk.

'No,' said Jaz. 'It was more like this.' She did an even sillier walk.

'I don't walk like that!' I protested. 'Do I, Burt?'

'No,' he said. 'It was more like this.'

And he did the silliest walk yet. Then George did one and then Billy. You wouldn't believe how silly Billy can walk when he wants to.

'That's enough!' said one of the parent helpers.

We all started walking sensibly.

'What did you buy when you sneaked off?' asked George.

I shared the chocolate bars and crisps

out between Burt, George, Billy and me. And
then I had to give Angela, Mia and Jaz some
to keep them quiet about the fact they'd
noticed me sneaking off.

Then I offered everyone a maggot. You
should have seen the faces of the parent
helpers. You should have heard the girls
scream.

'Dougal Daley!' shouted Mr Truss, from
the front. 'Come up here where I can keep
an eye on you.'

I went up to the front where all the
boring kids were.

'What are you carrying in that bag?'
asked Mr Truss.

'My lunch,' I said.

'Let me see.' He made me open the
bag. 'Are you really going to eat a football
covered in maggots for lunch?'

Can you believe he threw my bag away in a bin, football, maggots and all?

'We can't have maggots on a school trip,' he said. 'Health and safety.'

'But they are very healthy maggots!' I protested. 'And they were perfectly safe in my carrier bag!'

'One more word from you, Dougal Daley, and you will be staying in at break for the rest of term.'

I was about to protest, then remembered that would mean staying in at break for the rest of term.

OCKLESFORD GAZETTE

BEWARE OF FORGED £20 NOTES!

FOLLOWING THEIR WARNING IN LAST WEEK'S GAZETTE, POLICE ARE NOW WARNING OCKLESFORD RESIDENTS NOT TO USE £20 NOTES, AFTER SEVERAL FORGERIES WERE PASSED ON TO SHOP OWNERS TODAY. 'JUST WHEN WE THOUGHT WE'D SOLVED THE PROBLEM OF THE £10 FORGERIES, WE NOW HAVE A LOAD OF WORTHLESS £20 NOTES,' SAID MRS ALI OF NIPPY NEWS. FROM NOW ON, WE ARE ONLY GOING TO TAKE £5 NOTES.' The POLICE AGREE THAT THIS IS A GOOD IDEA. FROM NOW ON, PLEASE USE £5 NOTES ONLY WHEN OUT SHOPPING.

I have sent an email to Mr Sanderly, asking for payment in £5 notes. And one to Claude, telling him I'd pay him four £5 notes when he's done 20 envelopes. I hope he is counting.

My BriLLiaNT PLan

This email has just come in from Mr Truss:

To: Dynamo DD >

From: Egbert Truss >

I would like to formally terminate my contract with you and Igor the cleaner. His cleaning is terrible and he keeps leaving padded envelopes lying around. I found one under the sofa when I was checking whether he'd cleaned under it. I found one under the bookcase when I was checking there. I found one behind the toilet (which he hadn't cleaned very well at all). Please tell him that, if he doesn't collect them, I will destroy them.

I sent an email
to Igor Meerkat.
Here is his reply:

To: Dynamo DD >

From: Igor Meerkat >

I take my flowery apron and my feather duster and I go live in Albania until you stop send me these emails.

I emailed Mr Sanderly. Here was his reply:

To: Dynamo DD >

From: Elwitz Sanderly >

I did not find a cleaner for the teacher's house. He probably left the envelopes lying around himself. Don't talk to me about it again. Yes, I will pay you in £5 notes.

There was only one thing I could do — go and clean Mr Truss's house myself. With a bit of help.

I messaged George, Billy, Burt and Claude:

Me

You wanted to earn some money, right? Igor the cleaner was useless, so we are all going to clean Mr Truss's house tomorrow. I will pay you £10 each, in £5 notes.

18:05

Here are the replies:

Billy

We have school tomorrow.

18:06

Me

Don't worry – I'll write notes for you all!

18:07

Billy

You can't write a note for me – Dad will know.

18:08

Claude

Who will send the note in, if you're not at school?

18:09

Me

Claude, you are brilliant! Billy will go to school and take all our notes in.

18:10

Burt

But Mum will make me go to school.

18:11

Me

I will do a note to give our parents, saying we have a day off.

18:12

Once I'd sorted that out, I sent an email to Mr Truss.

To: Egbert Truss >

From: Dynamo DD >

I am terribly sorry that your house was not cleaned to your satisfaction. But don't worry, I have found a whole TEAM of expert cleaners! They will blitz your house while you are at school tomorrow (Tuesday) and when you come home, you will not believe how amazingly clean and tidy it is.
Please leave your key under the geranium. If you are satisfied with the job, please leave £80 plus £10 for my fee on Wednesday for me to collect while you are at school. It took me a long time and made Mum and Dad worry about how quiet I was being, but it was worth it.'

Regards

Dynamo DD – builder of phenomenal websites and the best goalie ever

Then I had to do letters for George, Burt, Claude and me. And one for our parents.

127 LONG ROAD
OIKLESFORD
MIDDX
(SHORT FOR MIDDLESEX)

DEAR MR TRUSS,

WE THE PARENTS OF GEORGE QUICKLEY,
CAN'T POSSIBLY SEND HIM TO SCHOOL
TODAY. SCHOOL IS FAR TOO BORING
FOR GEORGE, SO WE ARE GOING TO
KEEP HIM AT HOME.

YOURS SINCERELY,

MR & MRS QUICKLEY

14 ODDS AVENUE
OCKLESFORD
MIDDX
(SHORT FOR MIDDLESEX)

DEAR MR TRUSS

I AM TERRIBLY VERY DEEPLY SORRY THAT OUR LOVELY SON,
BURT IRONSIDE, CAN'T COME TO SCHOOL TODAY. HE HAS
BEEN UNDER A LOT OF PRESSURE LATELY, TRYING TO DO
THESE AWFUL HOMEWORK SHEETS FROM SCHOOL.

LAST NIGHT, IN DESPAIR, HE DECIDED TO EAT HIS HOME-
WORK SHEET. IT HAS MADE HIM VERY ILL.

COULD YOU PLEASE USE MORE INTERESTING HOMEWORK
SHEETS IN FUTURE? EVEN BETTER, WHAT ABOUT NO HOME-
WORK AT ALL, SO THE BOYS CAN ENJOY PLAYING FOOTBALL
INSTEAD?

YOURS SINCERELY

MR MRS Ironside

MR AND MRS IRONSIDE

PS MIGHT WE SUGGEST YOU CONTACT THE EXCELLENT
DYNAMO DD FOR ADVICE ON HOW TO MAKE SCHOOL MORE
INTERESTING?

1 Dipp Street
Ocklesford
Middx
(Short for Middlesex)

Dear Mr Egbert Truss,

I regret to inform you that Claude
can't come to school today because he
needs to spend the day trying to find
the shoe that floated down the
River Ockle when he tried to wash
dog poo off it.

I can't let him come to school
with one shoe.

Yours very politely,
Bianca Barleycorn
(Claude's Mum)

13 Makepeace Avenue
Ocklesford
Middx
(short for Middlesex)

Dear Egbert

It has come to our attention that our dear son, Dougal
Daley, is very fed up and bored at school. Dougal is a
very bright boy and a rising football star. It is no good
him being bored and fed up at school.

We are going to keep him at home until you make school
more interesting.

Yours sincerely

Christabel Daley   *Raymond Daley*

Christabel and Raymond Daley
(Parents to the best son in the world – and the worst daughter)

OCKLESFORD JUNIOR SCHOOL

Duty Road, Ocklesford, Middx

Dear Parents/Guardians

There will be no school tomorrow. We have a training day, to try and train our teachers to be more interesting.

We will be learning how to:

- Let the children play football wherever and whenever they want
- Let the children bring whatever lunch they want to school
- Let the children be as loud as they like
- Let the children do whatever they like, regardless of health and safety.

Yours sincerely

Mr E Truss

(short for Egbert Truss)

Isn't that the most brilliant plan ever? It's so brilliant that I ate my brown goo with a smile on my face instead of a grimace. My parents wondered what was wrong with me.

'Nothing's wrong with him,' said Sibble. 'He's just being his normal freaky self.' She said this while the juice from Mum's brown goo went between my smiling teeth and dribbled down my chin. But I was too excited to care.

I put my plan into action as soon as Mum was washing up. I waved my expertly forged note in front of her and told her we had a day off school tomorrow.

'Why couldn't school have mentioned this before?' she said. 'What are you going to do?'

'We're all going round to Billy's,' I said.

'Oh, good,' she said. 'Rather his house than mine.'

The first part of my plan was done. Now I had to wait until everyone was asleep, before sneaking downstairs to print off the notes for Mr Truss. It made a bit of noise, but it didn't matter. Mum and Dad just thought it was the noises from next door. When they found me half-way up the stairs, I told them that I'd been woken by the noises as well. Luckily, they didn't notice the letters that I'd hidden up my pyjama top.

They were right about the noise. It's a sort of grunting, groaning sound, and it definitely comes from the Witzel house. I remembered the big box Mrs Grim saw being delivered there. I

hope it's not another stolen creature.
I think I might have to investigate – after
I've earned some money at Mr Truss's
house.

I was up nice and early, so I could meet
Billy on the way to school.

'Why are you up so early, when there's
no school today?' asked Mum.

'Because there's no school today,' I
said.

'Well, you can take the dog for a walk
then.'

As soon as he heard the word 'walk',
the dog went mad, jumping around in circles,
whining, wagging his tail and barking. He
always does that. The only way to shut him
up is to take him for a walk. Mum went
back to reading her paper. I couldn't help
noticing the headline:

OCKLESFORD GAZETTE

Urgent message from the Police
BEWARE OF FORGED £5 NOTES!

FIRST WE HAD FORGED £10 NOTES. THEN WE HAD FORGED £20 NOTES. NOW WE HAVE HAD SEVERAL CASES OF FORGED £5 NOTES HANDED OVER TO SHOPKEEPERS IN OCKLESFORD. 'THIS HAS TO STOP', SAID MR SPEEDY, OWNER OF SPEEDY SPORTS.

'I CAN ONLY ACCEPT COINS NOW AND THERE IS NOT ENOUGH ROOM IN MY TILL. THE POLICE MUST DO SOMETHING AND QUICK!' 'WE ARE DOING SOMETHING,' SAID A SPOKESPERSON FOR OCKLESFORD POLICE. 'WE EXPECT TO MAKE AN ARRE VERY SOON.'

I was going to have to ask Mr Sanderly to pay me in pound coins from now on. But before that, I had to take the dog for a walk and clean Mr Truss's house.

I set off with the dog and my brilliantly forged letters, to meet Billy. Unfortunately, the dog thought the letters were for him and kept jumping up to grab them, so I had to scrunch them into my pockets. Then Billy was late.

'I had to stop Dad from driving me in,' he said. 'He thinks I'm not well and wanted me to stay at home. But I can't stay at home, because I have to deliver your forged letters.'

I must admit, Billy did look a bit pale. 'You could always come home once you've delivered the letters,' I said. 'Then you can help with the cleaning.'

'It's all right, thanks, I'd rather stay at school. Give me the letters.'

I pulled the letters out from my pockets.

'I can't give these to my dad!' said Billy. 'They're all scrunched up. And look at the envelopes — they've got your address on them!'

'Those were the only envelopes I could find,' I said, clinging on to the dog to stop him from biting Billy's hands off. But Billy was right. I'd found the envelopes in the recycling and they were addressed to Mum and Dad. 'Turn them inside out and hope he doesn't notice.'

By the time Billy went off with the letters, the dog was bored of trying to snatch them and had found something better to do — rolling in the river. He came out and shook thick, muddy water all over me. By the time he'd finished, I noticed that he had a log in his mouth, which he carried all the way home.

'You're not bringing that filthy dog and his muddy log into this house!' said Mum.

So I decided to bring him into Billy's house instead. When I arrived, George, Burt and Claude were already there.

'Why are you outside?' I asked.

'We don't know where the key is,' said George.

'It's under the geranium,' I said.

'What's a geranium?' asked Claude.

'No idea,' I said. 'And we can't ask Billy because he's at school.'

We all looked around, hoping for inspiration.

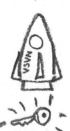

'Geraniums,' said Burt. 'I've definitely heard of them.'

'I'll Google it,' said George.

While we waited for him, the dog dropped his muddy log, lay down and started eating it.

'It's a flower,' said George.

We looked around for some flowers. The garden was full of them. It took us a long time to compare the picture on George's mobile to the flowers in the garden. None of them looked like geraniums, but we dug them up just in case. Even with the dog's help, we didn't find a key.

I sat down on the doorstep, next to a big pot with plants in it. 'Maybe we should climb in a window,' I said.

'Geraniums!' Burt shouted so loudly, I leapt off the step and I ended up sitting on the path. Burt was pointing at the pot.

He was right. The flowers in
the pot were geraniums. We
pulled them all up, with a bit
of help from the dog, but
found no key.

'Maybe he doesn't want
his house cleaned,' said George.
'Let's go play football on the field.'

That was the moment a car swerved
round the corner and screeched to a halt
outside Billy's house. It was also
the moment Claude picked
up the dog's muddy log.
The dog jumped up
to grab it back and
knocked over the plant
pot. It broke into
several pieces.

SMASH!

'Here it is!' I picked up the key, which was amongst the scattered pieces of pot. 'It was under the pot! Why didn't Mr Truss say so?'

'Why didn't Mr Truss say what?' A very stern, loud voice shouted up the path, followed by a very loud and stern Mr Truss, who'd just climbed out of the car that had screeched to a halt. 'Dougal Daley – what have you done now?'

Behind Mr Truss was a very pale-looking Billy. He had his hand over his mouth and was mumbling incoherently. I couldn't believe he'd ratted on us!

I glared at him. He tried to rush past me, but I wasn't going anywhere until he'd explained himself. Instead of explaining himself, he was sick all over my trainers. The sick looked a lot like Mum's brown goo.

Claude was still
wrestling with the
dog. 'That's not a
muddy log!' he cried.
'That's my school
shoe. You found it.
Well done and thank you,
Dougie's dog!'

That was when the police arrived.

GROUNDED AgaiN!

I, Dougal Daley, have been most unfairly
and cruelly grounded by my mean and unfair
parents. For the rest of my life. I am up in
my room, wondering how to escape, while my
mean and unfair parents think of a suitable
punishment for me.

It's the police's
fault. When they
turned up at Billy's,
the dog thought
they'd come to
play, so he jumped
up and put his muddy
paws all over their
nice clean uniforms —
they weren't very pleased.

the
pOLiCE's
FauLt!

'Are you the owner of this house?'
Sergeant Daramy glared at Mr Truss. 'And is
this your dog?'

Mr Truss stood there, looking down at
the plants pulled out and strewn about the
path, along with a lot of mud.

He should have hidden his key in a more
sensible place.

'Sir?' said PC Kim. 'We were called to
your house by a neighbour, saying some boys
were vandalising your garden. Is this true?'

'It was the dog!' I pointed at the dog.
He wagged his tail.

'It was Dougie!' Burt and George
pointed at me.

'I think the dog poo's all off my shoe,'
said Claude. 'It's just mud now.'

'Bleurrgghhhhh!' said Billy. He was being
sick again, but I dodged out of the way.

'I had to rush home from school with my son Billy,' Mr Truss explained. 'Because he was sick all over some notes he was trying to sneak onto my desk. Luckily, I drove in today instead of cycling, but I had to be quick or he would have been sick in my car.'

'Why aren't these boys at school?' asked Sergeant Daramy.

'We have a day off,' said Claude. 'While the teachers make school more interesting.'

'That is not true,' said Mr Truss. 'I am in the unfortunate position of being their teacher and I know there was school as normal today. But not for these boys.' He took out his mobile and called school. 'I would like you to contact the parents of George Quickley, Burt Ironside and Claude Barleycorn. Don't bother to contact Dougal Daley's parents as the details on the school records are false. I have a better way of making sure they know what he's done. No, you won't believe what he's done — it is even worse than when he brought his dog into school during pet week.' He listened for a while. 'Yes, it's worse than that. And that.'

When he'd finally decided which of my activities were worse than others, he turned to the police. 'Dougal's father is a window cleaner. Might I suggest that you drive around until you find him? And, when you do, tell him that Dougal is in very serious trouble — again.' He looked at me. 'Just what do you think you were doing this time?'

'What we agreed,' I said. 'I brought my team round to clean your house.'

'Clean my —?' His face went all red.

'Because Igor Meerkat didn't do it

properly. You owe me £80. Plus £20 for finding someone to do it.'

Mr Truss went even paler than Billy. 'I had an arrangement with a website, called —'

'Dynamo DD's Phenomenal Services,' I finished for him, as he seemed to have a bit of difficulty speaking. 'That's me — Dynamo DD.'

'But that was not your work,' said Mr Truss. his voice all quivery. 'The Making School Interesting website was yours — much more like the low standard I'd expect of you.'

'Thank you,' I said. 'I did my best. Are you sure you don't want some of my interesting homework sheets at £10 each?'

Mr Truss made a funny noise.

'£5 each?' I offered.

He looked like he was going to fall over, but PC Kim caught him. 'Are you all right, sir?'

'Just take him away,' groaned Mr Truss. 'Please.'

That's how I found myself being driven around by the police. They called me *young man* and told me I had a very badly behaved and muddy dog. 'He's not muddy now,' I said, which was true. While he was wriggling around, barking and slobbering the windows, all the mud had rubbed off him.

'You should find someone to clean the inside of your car,' I said. 'In fact, I know a very good website called Dynamo –'

I didn't manage to finish, as the car swerved round a bend and screeched to a halt, right outside Mrs Dogan's house. Dad was cleaning her upstairs windows.

It's not my fault Dad had such a fright when he saw the police that he dropped his bucket. It's not my fault the police ended up covered in soapy water. But, as usual, I was blamed for everything.

And now my mean and unfair parents have decided that, while I'm grounded I can make myself useful and clear out the understairs cupboard.

You would not believe how much stuff you can cram into an understairs cupboard. I've been at it for two hours and I've managed to fill the whole house with the rubbish that has come out of it. And you will absolutely not guess what I found in there.

The key to the Witzel house! It was lying on the floor. It must have fallen out of one of Mum's many handbags. I thought I might give it back to her in return for not grounding me after all, but I kept it for later use instead. That's because I found something else in there as well. You will not believe what it was.

A big old coat, a furry hat, a flowery apron and a feather duster. Last seen worn by Igor Meerkat.

To: Igor Meerkat >

From: Dynamo DD >

I have decided to come and live in Albania with you. I will bring over your flowery apron, old coat and feather duster, which I found in our understairs cupboard. I'm looking forward to telling Mr Truss who his cleaner really was.

Text from Dad:

OK, you are ungrounded.

My reply:

And I want double money for cleaning the car.

His reply:

Don't push it.

Message from Claude:

Claude

Mum is going to take me to the doctor to-morrow, because she says I've been acting strange. I won't be able to stay in for your envelopes. Can you do it instead? The key is under the gnome.

22:03

Just as well I've been suspended from school, while they decide what to do with me. That means I can go to Claude's and do the envelopes. I don't think making another forged note would work now.

At breakfast Mum and Dad had a big row about why I'd been let near the understairs cupboard and why Dad had ungrounded me when I was in the biggest trouble ever. They also had a row about who was going to stay at home to look after me. I told them I could look after myself. They told me to be quiet and take the dog for a walk.

I took the dog over the fields and told him he was in no circumstances to go in the river. He went straight in the river.

By the time I hauled him out, and made myself very wet and muddy, I had to go

straight to Claude's house to wait for
the envelope. I arrived in time to see
Claude leaving with his mum and little sister.
I hoped they wouldn't see me, but the dog
likes Claude and decided to bound up to him
— with me attached to the other end of
his lead.

'Hello, Dougal,' said his mum. 'I'm taking
Claude to the doctor. You'd better stay
away in case he's contagious.'

I carried on walking past
his house and only doubled
back when they were well
out of the way. I found
the key under the gnome
and let myself in.

I would rather not think
about what happened next.

PAddED EnveLOpE

I hid behind the curtains in Claude's front room and peeked out until I saw a shadowy figure coming up his path.

HOOdiE

Jeans

He was wearing jeans and a hoodie, so I couldn't see his face, but there was something familiar about the way he walked. He dumped the envelope, tapped a very poor version of Match of the Day on the door and walked briskly away.

When I say 'envelope', it was actually a huge padded envelope, stuffed full so it bulged. I reached down to pick it up.

That was the moment the dog decided to stop sniffing around Claude's front room and eating things he shouldn't. He rushed past me, grabbed the envelope and ran out of the door. With me chasing after him. I can run fast, but when the dog has something you desperately want, he's much faster. By the time we reached the fields, he was so far ahead of me that he had plenty of time to rip open the envelope and was munching his way through the contents by the time I arrived.

The envelope was full of whopping fifty pound notes!

At least it had been until the stupid dog ate them..

But I managed to rescue four of them — two from his jaws, one from under his muddy paw and another one that had landed in a puddle. Then I dragged the dog back to Claude's house.

As soon as we were back at Claude's, the dog realised he hadn't checked out upstairs, so he went straight up while I found his lead. By the time I'd gone upstairs to put it on him, he was happily going through the dressing-up box and eating a plastic sword. As I went to grab him, I heard a big loud bang on the front door. Followed by another bang, and another.

The dog ran downstairs, barking. I peeked out of the window and saw a shadowy figure banging on the door. After a few more bangs, I realised he was banging a terrible version of Match of the Day.

He'd come to collect the envelope!

I grabbed the first thing I could to disguise myself and cover my face. Then

I found a homework sheet and pen on Claude's desk on which to write a note:

Here is ALL that rEMAins of the pAddED EnveloPE. The rest is in the dog.

I went downstairs, being very careful not to trip over the Snow White cloak I was wearing. Even though it was hard to see through the Happy dwarf mask, I found what was left of the envelope and put the note I'd written in it. I opened the door a tiny crack. A hand came through, waving a £50 note.

Mr Sanderly must be so pleased with my envelopes, he's decided to pay me even more! I took the note just before the dog got hold of it and managed to stuff the remains of the padded envelope into the hand before the dog bit it — he thought it was very interesting. I slammed the door quickly, heard a grunt from the other side and then footsteps going away.

I decided to leave before he read my note.

On the way home, my mobile was buzzing so much I nearly dropped it. I had messages from everyone.

George

You won't believe this – the police came to school today – and arrested Mr Truss!

11:01

Burt

You should have been in school – Mr Truss was arrested!

11:02

Claude

The doctor said I was as normal as I could be so Mum took me straight to school. Mr Truss has been arrested!

11:03

Billy

Dad has been arrested. When they took him away, I heard him muttering your name. You don't know anything about it, do you?

11:04

I couldn't believe it. Mr Truss has been arrested and I missed it! But Mum had the radio on and I heard it on the local news. This is what the newsreader said:

An Ocklesford teacher, Mr Egbert Truss, has been arrested. First of all, police stormed his house and found several large padded envelopes, stuffed with forged £20, £10 and £5 notes, the very ones that have been used in shops in Ocklesford – the ones with 'made in Albania' under the Queen's head. Then the police went to Ocklesford Junior School and arrested Mr Truss.

Mr Garcia, headmaster of Ocklesford Junior School, was so shocked that he has closed the school until further notice.

Mr Truss is protesting his innocence. He says the envelopes found at his house weren't his. He said they were left there by his cleaner. The police refuse to believe this as they know teachers can't afford cleaners.

If the public have any information, there will be a reward.

Unbelievable. Mr Truss is a crook!

I was still grinning and shaking my head when an email came in from Mr Sanderly.

To: Dynamo DD >

From: Elwitz Sanderly >

Give back the money that was missing from the envelope.

Here's my reply:

To: Elwitz Sanderly >

From: Dynamo DD >

Your money is in the dog.

He replied straight away:

To: Dynamo DD >

From: Elwitz Sanderly >

You have until tomorrow to remove the money from the dog, or replace it. £2000 in £50 notes. At a new secure address.

Two thousand pounds! Where am I supposed to find that? I can't take it out of the dog – it would cost more than that to have him cut open by the vet and no way am I trying to find it when it comes out of the other end.

I was wondering what to do when another enquiry came in through the website. It was from the police!

To: Dynamo DD >

From: Ocklesford Police Station >

Please present yourself to Ocklesford Police Station as soon as possible. We will not pay you £10 for turning up.

PC Kim and Sergeant Daramy

I replied straight away:

To: Ocklesford police Station>

From: Dynamo DD >

I can't come – I'm in Albania with Igor Meerkat.

I didn't tell them Igor Meerkat was my dad.

The Angry CREaTure NExT DOOr

I didn't sleep very well last night. I was kept awake by thoughts tumbling about in my head. Mr Truss arrested. The police want to talk to me. The dog ate the money in the envelope and I had to find a way to replace it.

Another thing that kept me awake was the racket coming from next door. It really did sound like an angry creature in a cage. I decided to go round first thing and rescue it.

I had just managed to fall asleep when I was cruelly awakened by the sound of banging on my door, to the tune of Match

of the Day. Envelope Man had found me! I hid
under the duvet. The banging grew louder.
I put my fingers in my ears. Now it sounded like
a herd of elephants coming into my room, all
stamping to the tune of Match of the Day.
Then my duvet was ripped off me.

It wasn't elephants. It wasn't envelope
man. It was Billy, Claude, Burt and George.
They all looked very cross.

'It wasn't my fault!' I said, just in case.

'Dad thinks it is,' said Billy. He had his
arms crossed. So did the others.

'What was my fault?' I asked.

They sat on my bed, pinning me in with
the duvet. 'We want to know where you got
all the forged money from,' said Burt.

'What forged money?' I asked.

'The forged money in the envelopes
found in our house ,' said Billy.

'But it wasn't me!' I protested.

'I know,' said Billy. 'Dad says no way are you capable of coming up with such good forgeries. But you have been dealing with padded envelopes – just like the ones the police found at our house.'

'Claude does the envelopes,' I said.

'Could you describe the envelopes please, Claude?' said Billy.

'They are big, padded envelopes, that are delivered to the tune of Match of the Day,' said Claude. 'Half an hour later, they are collected to the tune of Match of the Day, in return for money.'

'We have to prove that Mr Truss is innocent,' said Burt.

'Why?' I asked. I like the idea of Mr Truss being behind bars – that would make him much more interesting.

'Because he's Billy's dad,' said George.

I suppose he had a point. I wouldn't want my dad behind bars — who would I beat at FIFA then? Besides, I was looking forward to putting Mr Truss in my home for old teachers.

'All right,' I said. 'I will help you with your enquiries. But first you have to help me. I need to go next door and rescue a poor creature.'

'Mrs Grim's got a poor creature?' asked Burt. 'I thought she just had a big cat.'

'And her husband has a guide dog,' said George. 'But he's very well looked after.'

'Why does Mrs Grim's cat need rescuing?' asked Claude.

'It's not that next door,' I explained. 'The noises are coming from the Witzel house.'

'I'm not going in the Witzel house,' said George.

'It would be breaking and entering,' said Billy. 'That's against the law.'

'Not if you have a key,' I said.

'How come you have a key?' asked Burt.

'I found it,' I said. 'After Mum lost it and had another one made. But I think it would be a good idea if you all sneak round the back, just in case.'

Mum was reading the paper in the kitchen and didn't notice that only four of us went past to go out into the garden. But she did give Billy a sad look. She went back to her paper and didn't notice them sneaking through the gap in our fence.

While they did that, I sneaked round the front, with my very best sneaking walk.

'What are you up to?'

I did a spectacular leap into the air. Mrs Grim was right behind me.

'I'm practising,' I said. 'For the school play.'

'Are you playing the part of a cat burglar?' she asked.

'No,' I said. 'Just an ordinary burglar.'

'Is your mum in?'

'She's working from home and very busy,' I said. I didn't want her going round and telling Mum I was sneaking around like a cat burglar.

'Your dad?'

'He's trying to clean windows.'

'Shouldn't you be at school?'

That's the thing with Mrs Grim, she never stops asking questions. 'No school today, because our teacher's been arrested,' I said.

'Oh, terrible business,' she said. 'Terrible. They just can't find the staff these days. They'll be having the kids forging money in class next. He didn't make you do that, did he?'

'Er, no, we had to make mousemats,' I said.

'Terrible business,' she said. Then she went home, thank goodness. But I had to carry on with my silly walk up and down the drive until she'd gone in. Then I dashed to the Witzel house and let myself in.

The last time I'd been in this house, it was full of pale carpets and posh furniture. Now it was empty. The only sound was someone quietly tapping Match of the Day on the back door. Followed by someone tapping Match of the Day a bit louder. Followed by several people tapping, and someone singing the tune.

I opened the back door before they had the rest of the neighbours wondering what was going on.

'We thought you'd forgotten to let us in,' said George.

'Or done a runner,' said Burt.

'I had to get rid of Mrs Grim,' I said.

'At least all the curtains are shut,' said Billy. 'So no one can see us.'

'So no one will know that we're being eaten by a creature in a cage,' said Claude.

'Depends on how good the cage is,' said Burt.

We wandered around downstairs, but didn't find anything suspicious. Then we went upstairs. With the curtains shut, the house was all gloomy and creepy. The stairs creaked. It was great.

We went into the small bedroom at the front, but there was nothing in it except for piles of padded envelopes.

Padded envelopes? Did I say padded envelopes?

'Just what I need!' I said, grabbing one.

'That's stealing!' said Billy.

'Why do you want a padded envelope?' said George.

'Can I have one?' asked Claude.

'Can I have on as well?' asked Burt.

In the end, we took one each.

We took them into Mr and Mrs Witzel's old room. It was empty apart from the dents in the carpet left by their old furniture. And some mouse droppings.

There was only one room left. Stan's. And that's where we found the creature.

It was so large that it nearly filled the room, but it was hidden under a thick dusty sheet. It was completely silent.

'Do you think it's dead?' whispered Claude.

'Maybe it's sleeping,' said Burt.

'Go on, Dougie,' said George. 'You see what it is.'

I took hold of the sheet and pulled. It stuck. Billy, Burt and George helped me pull it off. Claude kept guard. But there was no creature in a cage under the cloth.

It looked like the school photocopier, only much bigger.

'I wonder what it does,' said Billy.

'It's a space-ship,' said Burt.

'Don't be daft,' said George. 'It's the wrong shape. And there aren't any aliens in it.'

'How do you know?' said Burt.

'What's this button for?' asked Claude.

Before we could stop him, he pressed the button. The machine burst into life, making us all jump. Then it started firing weapons at us!

'Run for your life!' screeched George. We raced downstairs and stood panting in the hallway. All except Claude.

'It's eaten Claude,' whispered Burt, his eyes all wide and staring. 'It's going to eat us next.'

Then it went quiet. We all looked at each other. With great care, we began to creep back upstairs. The moment the stairs creaked, we all stopped. Then we started up again. Even though we were undoubtedly entering the jaws of death, we had no choice — our friend was up there.

Unless he'd been eaten. But we had to be sure.

We had to stop three more times before we made it to the landing. There was an almighty roar. Then next thing we knew, we were all downstairs again. When the noise stopped, we stood staring at each other.

'I think it burped,' said Burt.

'It must have found Claude tasty,' said George.

'It's a machine,' said Billy.

'A boy-eating machine,' said Burt.

'We'll have to go back and see,' said Billy. 'Dougie, you go first.'

'Why me?' I didn't want to be eaten next.

'Because it was your idea,' said George. 'And you're good with creatures.'

It's true. But I'd never looked after a boy-eating machine before. 'I tell you what,' I said. 'We'll all go up together.'

So up we went. This time we couldn't hear the stairs creak because the machine was making so much noise. Then it stopped. We waited on the landing, in silence.

Billy spoke first. 'Claude?'

Then George. 'Are you there, Claude?'

Then Burt. 'Have you been eaten by the machine?'

I was about to say something, when Claude came out of Stan's old room. You will absolutely not believe what he was holding in his hands. Bundles of money! One hand was full of £50 notes and the other was full of £20 notes. He had a big grin on his face.

'I'm rich,' he said. 'I won't have to stay in for any more envelopes now.'

'I want some,' said Burt.

'Me too,' said George.

'No point,' said Billy. 'They're forged.'

We all groaned. Then we stopped groaning when we realised what Billy had just said. We went back into Stan's old room. The machine was sitting quietly in the middle of it, surrounded by heaps of money.

'Should we count it?' said Claude.

Billy went round the machine, examining it closely. It was big and grey and on the side it said *Made in Albania*. It had several buttons on it. 'Which buttons did you press?' Billy asked Claude.

MADE in ALBANIA

'These two,' he showed him.

Billy pressed the third button. The machine sprang to life, making us all jump.

But this time we didn't run away. We stood and stared as the machine started spewing out £5 notes. Then Billy pressed the button that said STOP. Then he pressed the fourth button and out came a load of £10 notes. Then he pressed STOP.

'This is where the forged banknotes have been coming from,' he said. 'And they have been passed to Claude in the padded envelopes from the room next door. All we have to do is go to Claude's house and wait for the next envelope. Then we'll know who's been doing this.'

'We can't go to Claude's house,' I said. 'Because the dog ate all the money in the last envelope.'

They stared at me. 'You knew what was in the envelope?' asked Billy.

'Only when the dog ate it,' I said. 'When

I went to Claude's house yesterday because Claude was at the doctor having his head examined.'

'Mum won't let me stay off school any more,' said Claude. 'So I can't do the envelopes.'

'But we're off today anyway,' said George. 'Because Billy's dad's in prison.'

'He's not in prison,' said Billy. 'He's helping the police with their enquiries.'

'I think we can help them more,' I said. 'I've had a brilliant idea.' They all groaned. Then they listened to my brilliant idea and decided that it was brilliant after all.

We went back to my house and sneaked up into my room. 'Do you think you boys could make less noise, I'm trying to watch day-time TV!' Mum called up the stairs. 'It's bad enough with all that noise from next door!'

As soon as we were in my room, I

opened up the box of Angela's red ants. I
dipped the stick in and then transferred
them to a padded envelope. I did this three
times while everyone watched. Then we
went back to the Witzel
house and stuffed
the envelope
with £50 notes
from the forgery
machine. Then I sent
an email.

To: Elwitz Sanderly >

From: Dynamo DD >

I have your money. Please collect it from No 15
Makepeace Avenue at your earliest convenience.

'Who's Elwitz Sanderly?' asked Billy.

'He's Chief Envelope Man,' I said. 'Now all we have to do is wait,' I said.

'How long for?' asked Claude.

'I'm hungry,' said Burt. 'Is there anything to eat here?'

'Can we go in the garden and play football?' asked George.

'Of course not,' said Billy. 'We need to hide all this money.'

'Why?' we all asked at once.

'Because, when Elwitz Sanderly or one of his minions comes to collect the envelope,' said Billy, 'what will they think if they find us here with all their money?'

That's when we heard a sound that froze us to the spot – the sound of a key opening the front door.

'Quick!' I hissed, picking up a bundle of money and stuffing it up my pyjama top, together with the padded envelope with the ants in. Everyone did the same, but without the ants. That is, they stuffed the money up their tee-shirts. I was the only one wearing pyjamas. While we were doing that, we heard voices downstairs.

'Come in, come in.' You won't believe who it was, trying to sound all polite and friendly — my mum!

'This is the hallway,' we heard her say. 'As you can see, it's quite spacious.'

We all stared at each other. 'Perhaps we could give them some money to go away,' whispered Burt.

'No point,' I whispered back, glumly. 'Mum'll want to know where I got it from. We'll just have to hide.'

It wasn't very easy squashing five boys behind a forging money machine. Every time one of us tried to hide, another one popped out the other side. When Burt tried to hide, we all popped out. Then we heard the sound of footsteps coming up the stairs. Just as well that was the moment I had a brilliant idea. 'Get under the cover!' I hissed.

We picked up the cover that I'd pulled off the machine and threw it over ourselves like a tent. 'Keep still!' hissed Billy.

'I'm trying to,' hissed George, 'But Burt's treading on my foot.'

'And mine,' I said, trying to wriggle my foot.

'And mine,' said Claude.

'I haven't got three feet,' said Burt. 'But I'll move them anyway.'

'Shhh!' warned Billy.

At the same time, we heard a man's voice. 'Did you hear something?'

'Nothing at all.' Mum's voice. 'Let me show you the bedrooms.'

We heard footsteps creaking away. Then there was a reshuffle while Burt sorted his feet out.

'Ouch!' hissed George. 'Burt's got his elbow in my face.'

'And his other one's in mine,' I said, with one eye closed — the one with Burt's elbow in it.

'And mine,' said Claude.

'I haven't got three elbows,' said Burt.

'Shhh!' warned Billy. 'They're coming back.'

At the same time, we heard a woman's voice, not Mum's. 'I think I heard something as well.'

'Oh, it's probably just the house creaking,' said Mum in her friendly posh voice.

'I hope your ants don't escape,' whispered George.

I wish he hadn't said that. As soon as he did, I'm sure I felt an itch. Followed by another one, and another.

'Stop fidgeting!' hissed Billy. 'Or our cover will fall −'

That was the moment Mum opened the door to let the couple in.

'− off,' finished Billy. As the cover slipped.

'Dougall' yelled Mum. 'What are you —?' A bundle of banknotes fell out from under my pyjamas. '– doing here?' finished Mum.

'We were just —'

That was when we heard a loud tapping on the front door — to the tune of Match of the Day.

'Someone's at the door,' said Claude.

'I'd better see who it is,' said Mum. While she was on her way downstairs, Burt stood up and the cover fell off everyone. Then we heard voices coming from downstairs.

'Hello, Lysander, how lovely to see you.' Mum still had her friendly posh voice on.

Lysander? There is only one person I know with a silly name like that: Lysander Witzel, Stan's dad and owner of this house. The last I heard, he was still on the run

from his crooky activities. 'And Stan —
shouldn't you be in school?'

'Stan is home educated,' we heard Mr
Witzel say.

'What's Mr Witzel doing here?' asked Burt.

'It's his house,' said George.

'Of course,' said Billy, slapping his head like
he'd forgotten something mega important.
'Lysander Witzel, I should have known.'

I didn't know what he meant — he's
always known this is Lysander Witzel's house.

We heard Mr Witzel ask Mum a question.
'Where's Dougal?'

'He's upstairs,' said Mum.

'Why did Lysander Witzel suspect I was
here?' I asked. 'And why did Mum confirm it?'

'Because he's Envelope Man,' said Billy.

'No,' I said. 'Envelope Man is called Elwitz
Sanderly.'

'I wish you'd told me that before,'
said Billy. He sounded really cross. 'Then Dad
wouldn't be in trouble with the police.'

'What are you talking about?' I asked.

'It's obvious,' said Billy. 'Because —'

Mr Witzel filled the doorway. He was wearing black jogging bottoms, a large dark hoodie and big sunglasses. Next to him, Stan stood there in black jogging bottoms, a large dark hoodie and big sunglasses. He looked just like a smaller version of his dad.

He looked suspiciously like the person who'd delivered the envelope to me at Claude's.

'What are you all doing in here?'
demanded Stan's dad.

'We came to see the house,' said the
man who'd come to look at the house.

'Dougal has an envelope for you,' said Billy.

I wished he hadn't said that. Much as I
wanted to see Mr Witzel with ants crawling
up his arm, I had to keep that envelope for
Envelope Man. But Mr Witzel snatched it
off me and stood there, glaring at me.

'Open it.' Lysander Witzel handed the
envelope to Stan.

Stan opened the envelope. We all
watched as Stan put his hand in. Then
we all watched as he brought it back out
again. 'Ouch!' We all watched as he looked
into the envelope in horror. 'It's full of
ants!'

We all watched as Mr Witzel snatched

the envelope to see for himself.

Angela's ants must have been very fed up in there, because they were now swarming out all over Stan and his dad. Stan and his dad were jumping up and down, stamping and yelling and trying to brush ants off them. That gave us the perfect opportunity to run downstairs, followed by the couple who'd come to look at the house. Unfortunately, we couldn't run out, because Mum was standing in front of the door with her arms folded and her *Dougal you are in so much trouble* face on.

Before I could explain myself, there was a loud bang on the door. It was just a bang, no tune. Mum opened the door.

'Sergeant Daramy and PC Kim, how lovely to see you.' She had her friendly posh voice on again, but it was sounding a bit worn out. 'How can I help?'

'We're looking for Dougal Daley,' said Sergeant Daramy.

'He lives next door!' I said, in my best disguised voice.

'Here he is!' Claude pointed at me. 'Is he in trouble?'

'We've come to ask him some questions about forged banknotes,' said PC Kim. 'We were going to knock on his door, but Mrs Grim said he was here.'

'They're upstairs!' I said, pointing to the landing, where Stan and his dad were still jumping about. 'But be careful of the ants, they haven't eaten for a while and are hungry.'

'What are you talking about?' said Sergeant Daramy.

'Let me explain,' said Billy. 'Lysander Witzel has been forging banknotes on his machine here at night and passing them on to Claude in padded envelopes. Then Stan collects them and leaves them in our house. They knew to find the key under the geranium because Dougie told them.'

'I didn't!' I said.

'This time it wasn't his fault,' said Billy. 'He thought he was getting someone to clean our house. He didn't realise that Lysander Witzel and Elwitz Sanderly are the same person. Dad didn't realise that Dynamo DD Services was really Dougal, because the website was far too good.'

I had no idea what he was talking about. But the police obviously did. They looked upstairs, just as Stan and his dad came running down, still trying to brush ants off them. We all stood back, because we didn't want ants on us.

PC Kim grabbed Mr Witzel. 'You are under arrest for – ouch! For producing – ouch – forged banknotes – ouch! – made in Albania and – help, I've got ants all over me!'

'So have I!' yelled Sergeant Daramy.

'Dougal!' said Mum, in her *you're in even bigger trouble* voice.

'Angela!' I cried.

'Stan – run!' yelled Mr Witzel.

'Who's Angela?' asked Sergeant Daramy. 'Stop them!' But it was too late. Stan and his dad were running off down the road, still trying to brush ants off them.

'I don't think we'll be buying this house after all,' said the lady who'd come to look at it.

'But it's a lovely house!' said Mum.
'It doesn't normally have these boys in it. Or the Police. Or poisonous ants.'

'All the same,' said the man, but I heard no more. That's because I was running round to our house to fetch Angela. I told her she was about to have a feast of ants, if she didn't mind eating them off the police.

She didn't mind at all. PC Kim and Sergeant Daramy sat there very quietly, while Angela crawled over them, snapping up ants. When she'd finished, I let her suck up ants from the floor. She had a great time.

When she was finished, Sergeant Daramy told me I had a lot of explaining to do.

Me?

OCKLESFORD GAZETTE

FORGER ON THE LOOSE!

THE MYSTERY OF THE FORGED BANKNOTES HAS BEEN SOLVED. THEY WERE BEING PRODUCED IN A HOUSE IN OCKLESFORD, USING A SOPHISTICATED FORGING MACHINE MADE IN ALBANIA. UNFORTUNATELY, THE POLICE WERE UNABLE TO APPREHEND THE PERPETRATOR OF THIS CRIME BECAUSE HE RAN OFF WITH POISONOUS ANTS ALL OVER HIM, TAKING HIS ACCOMPLICE WITH HIM. BUT HE HAS BEEN IDENTIFIED AS LYSANDER WITZEL, WHO IS STILL ON THE RUN FROM A PREVIOUS CRIME. THE PUBLIC HAVE BEEN ASKED TO LOOK OUT FOR A MAN WEARING DARK JOGGING BOTTOMS, A HOODIE, AND COVERED IN NASTY RED SPOTS.

HE IS LIKELY TO BE JUMPING ABOUT, SLAPPING HIMSELF AND SCRATCHING. HE WILL BE WITH HIS SON, WHO IS DESCRIBED AS BEING A SMALLER VERSION OF HIS DAD. "THOSE ANT BITES ARE VERY NASTY," SAID SERGEANT DARAMY. "HE CAN'T HAVE GOT VERY FAR."

THE FORGERY MACHINE HAS BEEN SEIZED BY POLICE AND IS NOW HELPING THEM WITH THEIR INQUIRIES. THE TEACHER, MR EGBERT TRUSS, HAS BEEN RELEASED WITH A WARNING ABOUT BEING MORE CAREFUL WHERE HE LEAVES HIS FRONT DOOR KEY. ONE OF HIS PUPILS, WHO CAN'T BE NAMED BECAUSE HE IS TOO YOUNG, HAS BEEN ASSISTING POLICE WITH THEIR ANT BITES.

I can't believe it — Mr Witzel has escaped yet again! But at least we won't be seeing him around for a while.

Billy has now spelt out to me how he knew that Elwitz Sanderly was really Lysander Witzel. When I say spelt out, I really mean spelt out. Because that's just what he did.

'What do you get if you take the name Lysander Witzel and rearrange all the letters?' he asked.

'An incorrectly spelt man,' I said.

Billy sighed. I don't want to alarm you, but when he sighed, he sounded a bit like Mr Truss. Then he took a piece of paper and wrote the letters of Mr Witzel's name like this.

LYSNDRWTZL
AEIE

Then he put them together again in a different order:

ELWITZ SANDERLY

'It's called an anagram,' said Billy. 'Why don't you have a go with your name?'

I stared at him. 'You're not turning into a teacher, are you?'

'No way do I want to be a teacher,' he said.

After that, Mr Truss came from the police station and took him home. As soon as he'd gone, I wrote my last ever email as Dynamo DD. I have decided that trying to make millions isn't worth the effort — I'd rather go and play football. Maybe one day I'll play in goal for Stamford United and earn millions doing that.

To: Egbert Truss >

From: Dynamo DD >

Dear Mr Truss,
It has come to my attention that you haven't paid me
for finding you a cleaner. Please could you pay me £10
in pound coins, as I don't want to have another forged
banknote. Also, did you know that your name is an
anagram of Sergers Butt?

I'm still waiting for a reply.

978-0-9956972-2-5

"I, Dougal Daley, am dead! Ok I'm not actually dead. But if I'm not careful I soon will be."

In this first book, football-loving Dougal Daley finds himself at risk from the mysterious creature living in the garden shed. Nobody believes him but as a precaution, he sets upon writing his will - rewarding those who help him and disinheriting those who get on his bad side. Meanwhile, as limbs and windows alike are broken by rogue footballs and unhinged canines, Dougal finds himself in all sorts of trouble. . .and NONE of it is his fault!

978-0-9956972-5-6

"Mum," I yelled. 'Sybil, the Goliath bird-eater spider, is no longer in my room!"

In this second book, football-loving Dougal Daley once again finds himself on the wrong side of almost everyone. Someone has stolen his pet tarantula, Sybil (named after his sister – they both have very hairy legs), and she (the spider, not the sister) is being held to ransom. Dougal must fulfill the kidnapper's demands before poor Sybil is tortured...one leg at a time!

And here are some more books to enjoy from Wacky Bee Books:

978-0-9956972-9-4

"Three Cherry Charm Sparkle Smoothies, please, with extra cherries. We've got a lot to discuss!"

At Twitch Magazine Veronica couldn't be more excited when she is given her first article to write: a feature on the most exciting band in Witch City, Double-Bubble. Things take a mysterious turn when Double-Bubble are kidnapped. Could Belinda Bullfrog from Twitch's rival magazing Nosy Toad be behind it all? Veronica and her friends must piece together the mystery of the missing girl band, resuce them and get Twitch Magazine's article back on track before it's too late!

978-1-9999033-0-5

Eleven-year-old Felix Twain's life revolves around the number two.

He skips every second step when he takes the stairs, taps door handles twice and positions objects in pairs. The problem has become so bad that Felix is on the verge of being expelled from school because the principal has had enough of trying to run the school around his very specific rules.

Then Charlie Pye arrives and turns his world upside down. She's grown up with very few rules. She eats cereal for lunch, calls a boat home, and has a very loose interpretation of school uniform. The question is, can Felix ever learn to be wrong when he is so obsessed with being right?!

978-0-9956972-8-7

"The girl and her dog sit eating salty liquorice on a half-built suspension bridge in the Amazon rainforest."

Elise is lonely. Her mum is far away in Brazil helping to finish the building of a suspension bridge and her dad is busy trying to get by as a musician in the Danish city of Copenhagen where they live. So when Elise asks for a dog to keep her company, her dad finds it hard to refuse. But the dog that Elise ends up with is no ordinary dog. He is second-hand, he looks like an ugly rabbit, he smells of cheese...and he can talk!